I0760699

Passion in an Improper Place

Other Books by Glenn Alan Cheney

How a Nation Grieves:
Press Accounts of the Death of Lincoln,
the Hunt for Booth, and America in Mourning

Love and Death in the Kingdom of Swaziland

Poems Askance

Thanksgiving:
The Pilgrims' First Year in America

Neighborhood News

Law of the Jungle:
The Tenharim People and Environmental Anarchy in Amazonia

Frankenstein on the Cusp of Something

Journey on the Estrada Real:
Encounters in the Mountains of Brazil

Journey to Chernobyl:
Encounters in a Radioactive Zone

Acts of Ineffable Love

Life in Caves

Just a Bunch of Facts

The Merry Burial Compendium

Passion in an Improper Place

Glenn Alan Cheney

New London Librarium

Passion in an Improper Place

by Glenn Alan Cheney

Published by
New London Librarium
Hanover, Conn. 06350
NLLibrarium.com

ISBNs

Hardcover:	978-1-947074-61-3
Paperback:	978-0-9856284-5-1
Ebook:	978-0-9798039-5-6

Printed in the United States of America

Chapter One

Gumballs

This is the truth of what happened to Ysa, Kit and Soong Tan in Amazonia. The reporters didn't get the whole story, not by a long shot. The American consulate in Belém released only the official information, which is to say nothing. The officials probably knew more than they reported. They didn't mention the rain of porpoises or anybody getting sawed in half or the three crude coffins, small, medium and large. They alluded to a plane crash but not as a cause of death. Nothing about a war.

If it were anyone else but Ysa, it would sound like a make-believe adventure movie, the kind made for TV. But somehow she really got herself involved in such situations. A couple of years ago, for example, she found herself going to Burma and parachuting out of an airplane disguised as a nun. But, quite un-nun-like, she knocked off the biggest drug lord in the world, rescued the prettiest little girl you ever saw, and ended up the arms of Mr. Perfect. He moved right in. They didn't get married, but they're shacked up like married people except that when they had sex they made love, too.

The little Dutch-Burmese girl, the green-eyed Soong Tan, went right into the sixth grade. Ysa got a job identifying microbes in a pathology lab. Kit quit his job as a not-for-profit commando and opened up an ice cream stand off Virginia Route 169. Kit's Kones. Incredible place. A hundred and forty-four flavors. Blueberry-mango. Guava and cheese. Cinnamon-pumpkin. Bourbon. Bourbon and cloves. Cloves and cranberries. You'd weigh five hundred pounds before you tasted all his flavors. People came all the way from Washington, sometimes even whole busloads of people. He had congressmen in there. Senators. Ambassadors. Generals. People came to have an ice cream cone just to see who else was having an ice cream cone. He'd have a whole mess of famous people sitting around picnic tables, licking their cones and blotting ice cream off their shirts. Kit made so much in the summer he could afford to take the winter off.

Last winter he got a call from his foster-brother. Edgar. The last guy in the world named Edgar. Edgar lived in Brazil, right on the mouth of the Amazon in a city called Belém. Edgar had a Brazilian wife named Elizama. Kit hadn't heard from Edgar in years. Now all of a sudden Edgar just had to talk to him. He had big plans. He was going to get rich. He wouldn't tell Kit what it was. He wanted him to come down to Brazil and see it first-hand. Kit said, "This better not be some Amway deal," and Edgar said, "Amway's nothing compared to this."

Well, it was a cold, rainy spring and Soong Tan had two weeks off for Easter and Ysa said she'd always wanted to see the Amazon. She packed safari shorts, half a dozen T-shirts, malaria pills, a blank diary book, a camera, binoculars for watching birds, a magnifying glass for weird insects, a little field microscope for tropical germs, a telescope in case there was an eclipse or something, a ten-pound first aid kit in case there was a war, enough other junk for Kit to consider taking a camel for their baggage. She called her friend, Susan, and said, "Can you watch my ferrets for a couple of weeks? I'm going up the Amazon."

Susan said, "The Amazon. Are you nuts?"

"I need to get away from civilization," she said. "Just for a while. I want to see how the planet used to be."

So the next thing you know, they're on their way. Varig Airlines down to Rio. Some rattletrap puddle-jumper up to Belém. Susan pictured it with vines and boa constrictors hanging off the wings. She could just see Soong Tan's round, Oriental face pressed up against the window, all wide-eyed and saying "Like, wow." But then a postcard from Ysa said it wasn't all that bad in Brazil. They were about halfway civilized, in the cities anyway. It was when you get out into the interior that you found your boa constrictors, anacondas, and pythons. Your alligators. Your piranha. Your malaria, yellow fever, elephantiasis, leprosy, jungle rot and everything else the human body can catch.

So of course Ysa went there. She wasn't worried. She had Kit.

She's also had the kind of looks that let a girl get away with murder. Being of Dutch-Norwegian stock, she had green eyes and yellow hair. Being the kind of person with a little discipline at the refrigerator, she kept her feisty little butt in shape. She was the kind who, when she smiled, everybody just trusted her and liked her. Guys started clowning around. Women wanted to tell her their problems. Kids wanted to tell her stories about their little lives.

Traffic cops let her go with a warning.

Yet she was nice. A regular person. She liked a cold beer on a hot day. She cut coupons. Sometimes her car didn't start. She got headaches.

Anyway, she and Kit and little Soong Tan made it to Belém without the plane crashing or anything. Edgar met them at the airport. They were two degrees south of the equator. The humidity was like something from dinosaur times but with garbage in the streets and a big outdoor fish market right downtown. Susan got a postcard that said it was like walking through clam chowder. Not that Ysa would ever break a sweat or anything. Not her. Not Kit. They looked like a deodorant commercial coming across the airport lobby, as fresh as a mouthful of Scope.

Edgar looked like Larry the Lounge Lizard in his flowery shirt unbuttoned halfway down his golden-brown chest and great gobs of 14-karat gold chain swinging around his neck. He was all over Kit with the handshakes and hugs and pats on the back. Ysa wrote in her diary that it felt like getting hugged by a reptile in a wet fur coat. He had yellow teeth and smelled like a half-empty cup of coffee that's been used as an ashtray. He had a kind of hatchet face with a nose that had steep sides and tall, deep nostrils which in certain light you could see up inside.

This was the first time Kit had seen him since Edgar left home and joined the Marines. Kit was just a foster kid in the house, three or four years younger than Edgar. The parents treated Kit like dirt. Edgar treated him like a gnat. So as soon as he could, Kit pulled an Edgar, except what he joined was the army. Edgar ended up being a cook at Parris Island. Kit ended up in Special Forces in Southeast

Asia.

But first thing at the airport, Edgar bellows out, "Yo, bro!" and starts with the Brazilian-style back-slaps.

Kit backs off for a conventional hand-shake and just says, "Hello, Edgar. Long time no see."

"Boy, you can say that again, little brother. When was it?"

"A good twenty years ago. You were seventeen and full of pimples and had the grubbiest little mustache I ever saw."

"Haw! Time sure goes by, doesn't it? I could barely remember what you looked like. I had this memory of somebody about four feet tall who needed his nose wiped."

"Well," Kit says, "it's been wiped."

"Haw, haw, haw!" More back-slaps. Edgar loves his little brother. Suddenly they've been the best of bros since day one. Kit keeps giving Ysa looks of complete disgust. When he introduces her, Edgar not only moves in for a real tight hug but also, she's sure, feels around for her bra strap.

She pulls away and turns his attention to Soong Tan.

"What a little cutie-pie," he says, pinching one of her chubby little cheeks. "Jeepers, creepers, where'd you get them peepers, kid?"

The source of her pretty green peepers was a long story. Ysa didn't go into it. She just smiled wanly and said, "So do you have a car here or what?"

Edgar takes them home in his Fiat. He's got a big apartment in a building that looks to Ysa like a concrete block with windows. The apartment's got four bedrooms plus a bedroom for the live-in maid. Edgar never finished high school, but he's got a live-in maid. He snaps his fingers and the maid comes running. He says, "A little more ice for my drink, Maria," and she brings it. Even if the house were on fire, he wouldn't have to drag his heels off the coffee table. He could just snap his fingers and say, "Maria, would you put out that fire, please?"

Susan got a postcard from Soong Tan written on one of those first days in Brazil. All it said was, "Dear Aunt Susan: It is incredibly boring here. Hot, humid and nothing to do. TV sucks here. Why did they bring me to such a place? I don't get it. Yours truly, Soong Tan."

Ysa sent Susan a letter describing Elizama, Edgar's wife. It fit the stereotype of Brazilian women. Very tan. Very bright red lipstick so powerful it stains her big white teeth. Very curvaceous body, especially around the rump. A little heavy on the hips, maybe, but she moved them around like a professional. Great gobs of black hair. Nails to die for. Matching toenails. Lots of flashy rings on all her fingers. Jeans meant for women who get lots of exercise. She had big dark eyes that stretched waaaay open when something amazed her and that narrowed down to the size of snake eyes when she had something dark and personal to say.

Elizama had the apartment decorated all weird with Umbanda stuff. Umbanda is weird religion that got brought over from Africa by the slaves. Then it mixed with Catholicism to create bizarre gods and goddesses named after the saints but in charge of things like the sea, the sky, bad luck, lightning, and stuff. When believers worship, they burn candles and incense and go into trances and sacrifice chickens and practice voodoo. Edgar and Elizama didn't believe in it. They just had the stuff for decoration all over their walls and hanging from the ceiling and lurking on whatnot shelves. They had swordfish bills, porpoise eyes, dried monkey feet, rattles made from bones. And crucifixes. No air conditioning. Just ceiling fans. A little breeze came off the river, which is about ten miles wide there. Sometimes a rain storm would pass by and cool things off a bit. Ysa and Kit just sat around the apartment feeling like a couple of damp rags. It took all their energy just to snap their fingers for Maria to bring more ice.

Edgar treated them well. Big meals. Tours of the town. Juices you've never heard of. Fresh Brazilian coffee in tiny little cups. Elizama took Ysa out to have her fingernails done right and her body hair waxed so she could go to the beach in one of the itsty-bitsy tangas they wear in Brazil. Dental floss, they call it. Because it gets down into the crack.

While Ysa was getting herself tuned up to Brazilian standards, Edgar took Kit to a whore house. Not a bordello or anything. Just a whore house. Plain as can be. It reminded him of the lobby of a college dorm back in the days when college was cheap. He said he was afraid even to touch the walls. The lobby was just plastic chairs and drunk guys sitting around waiting to get laid. The closest thing to a frill was a humongous gumball machine over in the corner. It was the kind that's six feet tall with flashing lights and a million gumballs. When you buy one it rolls down a long winding chute inside a clear column under the globe of gumballs. Kit found that very weird. He never seen a gumball machine like that, and he never imagined he'd first see one in Brazil. And on top of that, he wondered, who would go into a whore house for a gumball? He figured it was probably for the girls. Whores are always chewing gum, right? He'd never thought of it before, but it kind of made sense. A whore house would have to have a supply of gum. But it was weird, this big thing standing there in the corner like some kind of a Martian with a huge head full of multicolored brainballs.

Edgar makes like he practically owns the place. "Take your pick," he says, calling out a parade of girls who didn't look old enough to vote. "Vanilla. Milk chocolate. Licorice. We've got 'em all here. Twelve dollars each. Buy two, get one free." He wasn't talking gumball flavors. Kit backed off. He didn't need to hire a girl. He had Ysa. She was gorgeous. Hair the color of white corn. The prettiest face in the world and legs that bring men to their knees. Her breasts look like something off a marble statue. Kit wasn't going to mess with some chick who probably had more diseases than a hospital.

So Edgar says, "OK then, be a chicken, see if I care. I've got a little business to attend to with my sweetheart here –" and he strokes this half-naked teenager who looks like she just got off the boat from Africa. "If you want, you can go across the street and have a beer, I'll be there pretty soon. The word's *cerveja*."

And off went Edgar with his sweetheart. Kit had nothing against beer on a hot day, but before he went, he plopped a coin into the gumball machine, just to see how it worked. It took him a while to figure out which coin, but it turned out to be worth twenty-five cents, same as in America. He gives it whirl, and a yellow gumball drops down from the globe and starts down the chute, around and around and around. Something trips off a kind of a little siren, a pinwheel up on top spins around, whistling and shooting off sparks, and the yellow ball of gum pops out a little door down near his ankles and rolls across the floor. Kit almost fell down laughing. It was the fanciest gumball machine in the world, and there it was, in a grubby little whore house on the outskirts of the Amazon jungle.

So he's across the street drinking Brahma beer and trying to fit all this on a postcard when Edgar comes out with a great big smile on his face. Kit thought that was odd. Men don't usually smile when they're done with a whore. They're always sad. But Edgar's got this big grin across the front of his head. He sits down at the table with Kit – it's a little metal table out on the sidewalk, under a canopy – and signals for the waiter to bring another bottle of beer. Kit says, "You look mighty pleased with yourself, Edgar. Something tells me you're out at least twenty-four bucks."

Edgar just ignores that and says, "So whadja think?"

"I hope that's not the business you brought me here to see."

Edgar smiles up a big mouthful of crooked yellow teeth. Kit feels like smacking him with a chair. But then Edgar says just one word: "Gumballs."

Kit's taken aback. He almost spills beer on himself. Gumballs.

"I heard you try it out," Edgar says in a sly tone, as if he were talking about one of the girls. "You couldn't resist, could you."

Kit thinks about it. He supposes he could have resisted just fine. He's sure he will next time. It was twenty-five cents down the drain. A little entertainment, maybe, but once you've done it, well, as he wrote to Susan, "It's time to move on."

Bear in mind: Kit's been around the block a few times. He's parachuted behind enemy lines. He's flown helicopters. He was in on Ysa's mission into Burma. He climbed Mt. Blanc in bare feet. He did survival training in the Congo. He was in the Olympic try-outs for marksmanship. So if a gumball machine manages to get a quarter out of him just once, well it must be a pretty good machine. But it's going to have to fly around the room backward to hold his interest for long.

Edgar isn't holding his interest any better than a fancy gumball machine. Kit's already getting bored with him and his constant pressure. He's always saying, Come on, have another drink, or You know what y'oughtta do, y'oughtta buy some land here, or Do you have any idea how many square meters of frog skins this country produces in a year? It's a lot of pressure when the temperature's a hundred and three and the humidity's almost as high and the city buses sound and smell like Russian tanks and everybody's got their TVs turned up all the way and there's nobody else to talk to but Edgar.

Edgar signals for the waiter to bring him a pack of Hollywoods. The waiters here have white jackets. Kit likes that a lot. It reminds him of the French colonies in Asia and Africa. So far it's the best thing about Brazil, besides the gumball machines. The waiter brings Edgar's cigarettes, waits until Edgar has one in his mouth, lights it for him. Kit likes that, too. Edgar hardly seems to notice. He squints through the smoke but doesn't say anything while some kind of impact's supposed to be sinking into Kit. All Kit's thinking is that he could make a fortune in this country if he started a brewery and made beer out of something other than swamp water and rice.

Finally Edgar leans in close and says something. Kit can't hear it because a bus is going by. He leans in a bit to hear it better. This time, just as Edgar says it, a kid on the sidewalk lets loose with two-fingered whistle and shouts something to somebody on the other side of the traffic. Kit just smiles as if he heard what Edgar said and leans back.

"You didn't hear me," Edgar says in a moment of relative lull. He looks hurt.

"Say what?"

"I say that was my gumball machine."

Well that raises Kit's eyebrows a bit. His half-brother owns the fanciest gumball machine in all of South America and he's got it installed in a roach motel. And by the look on his face, he's as proud as the father of twin boys.

Kit says, "That's quite an asset. Hell of a good location." He can already smell what's coming. He's glad it won't be tempting.

"That's just one," Edgar says. "I've already got ten of them deployed all over Belém."

"In whore houses?"

"Not all of them. One in a supermarket. One at the bus station. You probably saw the one at the airport..."

Kit tilts his head pensively. He searches his memory banks for the image of a six-foot gumball machine or even the distant whine of a siren. "'fraid I missed it," he says.

"Yeah, the idiots who run the place put it over near the police kiosk. It's safe, but who's going to go near cops just for chewing gum?"

Edgar waits. It takes Kit a while to realize he meant it as a real question. He wanted an answer. Who goes near cops just for chewing gum?

"Oh, um, well...I don't know. Other cops, I guess."

"Wrong! The answer is nobody. It's a wasted asset. If you want to make money off a recreational flavored multi-chewable snack dispenser, you need traffic. In the United States, it has to be kids. In Brazil, hell, everybody's a kid. These Wiz-Bang machines – that's who makes them, Wiz-Bang, Ltd. – are like carnival waiting for a quarter. I average two hundred and seventy dollars a month per unit. Ten units is twenty-seven hundred per month. In a country like this, that's money. But now look: a hundred machines, twenty-seven thousand. Per month. You know what that adds up to in a year?"

Kit doesn't even bother trying to figure that out in his head. Edgar sits back with his cigarette, waiting for Kit's jaw to hit the sidewalk. But Kit's jaw remains locked. Finally, Edgar gives him the answer. "Three hundred and twenty-four thousand dollars. Per annum."

Kit whistles with disbelief and says, "That's sure a lotta gumballs." He knows what's coming.

Meanwhile, Ysa had two girls working on her nails at the same time. She was having them painted with rainbows on a background the color of watered-down Bordeaux.

Soong Tan was getting hers done the same way but quite against her will. She looked like she was getting her fingernails ripped out, not painted up. She came right out and expressed her opinion. "This is stupid," she said. "Even if they look like rainbows, it's unnatural. I bet it causes cancer."

"We'll just do it once," Ysa said. "For the experience. A little civilization to take with us into the jungle."

Elizama didn't hear any of this. She was under the hair drier. The few moments of solitude filled her head with things to say. As soon as she came out, she hit the ground running.

"Man in zis country, no good," she said. Her accent made her sound like a little girl. "I never marry wis Brazilian man. No way. Zey don't hispect you."

Ysa, half dizzy with the fumes of fingernail polish, said, "Is Edgar a good husband?"

"Oh, yes. He's good. He comes home at night. He talks to me. He always tell me his plans. He's soooo eentelligent."

Ysa hadn't detected much in the way of eentelligence in Edgar. As a matter of fact, she thought he was pretty dumb. And to her, he seemed the worst kind of dummy, the kind who thinks he's smart. Trouble was, he had irrefutable proof of his superior intelligence. He could beat just about anybody at just about any kind of board game or card game. He played Kit and Ysa in poker the same day they arrived and cleaned them of all their American coins. The next morning he whipped Kit's butt in chess. By afternoon Kit would play him in anything just because it gave him an excuse not to talk for a while. So Edgar beat him at Chinese checkers and then Crazy Eights and then backgammon. Kit knew his foster-brother was cheating just to see if he could do so undetected. He didn't care. At night they played a Brazilian card game something like gin rummy with a lot of extra rules. Pretty soon Ysa could tell Kit was just tossing in cards to get rid of them, handing Edgar vast combinations. Edgar beamed with joy as he clobbered everybody else by several thousand points. Smart dummy that he was, he couldn't see that no one else was even trying. Elizama didn't seem to notice much either. She never shut up.

Nor did she shut up at the beauty salon. Watching the work on

Ysa's nails as if they might end up in a museum, she gave a detailed report on the errors and inadequacies of Maria, the maid. Maria had failed to clean behind a certain toilet where Edgar tended to mark his territory. Maria bought wilted collard greens at the market. Maria always came back late after her day off. Maria neglected to fill the ice tray. Maria had fleas.

Ysa never knew what to say to Elizama. She tried to maintain a look of sincere concern, but when it came time to contribute to the conversation, she found her brain devoid of any possible offering. Once she managed to ask what Edgar did for a living. Elizama answered, "He has a booziness."

"A booziness?" She had no idea how one could earn a living at that. "What kind of booziness does he have?"

"Oh, I don't know. In Portuguese, we call it *negócios*."

Then Ysa understood. *Negocios* meant business. It sounded like the Spanish. That was how she was learning Portuguese. Every time a word sounded like the French or the Spanish, both of which she spoke, she learned it. This would come in handy later, out in the jungle, when things got serious.

Once they got their bodies all tuned up, Elizama took Ysa and Soong Tan to the beach. Ysa thought she was gazing out over the Atlantic until she swam and discovered it was fresh water. That vast expanse of sea was the Amazon itself.

The sun burned down from directly overhead. Ysa kept slathering on the Number 15 sun screen, but she still felt herself burning. When she asked Elizama to pass the sunscreen, Elizama reached over to squirt a blob into the palm of her hand. But rather than squirt, she gasped. Her index finger, with its incredibly long rainbow-streaked nail, darted to Ysa's palm and jabbed into a place just below the middle fingers. With eyes so wide her eyeballs almost fell out, she looked up at Ysa and said, "*Meu Deus!*"

At first she thought the pedicure girls must have done something to her hand, but then Elizama leaned in real-real close and poked the tip of her nail into a crack in Ysa's palm.

"Are you seek?" Elizama asked.

Except for the effects of the sun and some lingering dizziness from the morning of nail polish fumes, Ysa felt fine. She said, "No, I'm not sick...not that I know of."

"Is somebody in your family very hich?"

"Very hich?"

"Hich. Much of money. No?"

Ysa shook her head. No rich people in her family. No family, in fact. Her father was killed in Burma. Her mother died of cancer. No brothers, no sisters. She thought she had an uncle in Netherlands who worked in a bank, but she didn't even know his name. "Does it say I'm sick?" she asked, squinting into her palm.

"*It says you die,*" Elizama whispered, looking up with wide-eyed wonderment. "But hich. You die, but vehy, vehy hich when you go."

Chapter Two

The Plan

But Ysa didn't believe that stuff. She was too rational. Susan had taken her to see a psychic once, back in Virginia, before Burma. Moi was her name. Moi told Ysa she was going to fall in love within a year. She told her she was going to have a child. She told her she was going to take a long trip to a warm place. And it all came true. She met Kit. She adopted Soong Tan. She went to Burma, and now Brazil. But Ysa still didn't believe it. She said that could have happened to anybody. Like everybody dressed up like a nun armed with a semi-automatic weapon and parachuted into Burmese jungles to inject drug lords with deadly diseases.

Elizama was a psychic, too. She read palms. She did Tarot. She saw the future. She looked at Ysa's palm and knew she was going to die and then become very rich. She saw a flock of parakeets and knew Kit was going to leave her for another woman and then become an angel. She looked at the last bit of coffee in a cup and knew Soong Tan was going to be alone for a long, long time, with danger lurking around her like jackals. Entrails in a butcher shop window showed her coffins headed for the sea.

That night, the same night Ysa got her nails done and Kit heard the Gumball Plan, they were in bed, maximizing their appreciation of human perspiration. As Ysa wrote to Susan, "When you're in Amazonia, you do as the Amazonians do. You sweat. You get into it. It's good for you. It cleans the pores. It cycles water through the body" They were in bed cycling a lot of water through their pores. Kit was fascinated with the dental floss lines of Ysa's new sunburn. Ysa didn't mind the attention at all, his fingers and lips walking the fine line between gringo winter-white and equatorial Brazilian tan. She was fanning the fire, licking the sweat off him, off just the right spots. He was doing the same. They licked sweat until the salt got the better of them. Then they drank vodka tonics. Then they licked more sweat from more places, which of course just got them sweating more.

Ysa paused from her lingual exploration of his thigh and said, "Do you think it's possible to tell the future?"

Kit said, "I think I'm going to love you forever. Care to take a bet whether it's true?" He pulled her up and licked a swath from her collarbone to her ear.

"No bet," she said in a close-up hush, kissing the dampness from his earlobe. "But that's not what I mean. I mean can the lines on your palm tell you how long you're going to live?"

Kit just chuckled. "I can see how maybe....just maybe something about your palms can hint at your health fifty years down the road. Maybe. But how could they possibly know that ten years down the road you're going to get run over by a bus?"

As soon as he said it, Ysa started thinking about bus accidents. She saw herself stepping into the street, looking left as from the right a bus came barreling along, the wrong way down a one-way street – illegal and unlikely, but that's how accidents happen. Especially in Brazil. She had no trouble imagining it. She could see little Soong Tan, her pinched, round oriental eyes in her own father's chubby Dutch face, eyes and face both gaping to take in the impossible scene of her big sister dead in the street, not believing it, suddenly gushing with tears as she rushes to her sister's crushed body. Suddenly she's alone again, on the street, defenseless, this time in a country foreign to the foreign country she moved to from Burma. In this irresistible nightmare that Ysa kept having – having in a dozen different forms – somebody eases Soong Tan from her fallen sister, leads her under a protective arm to a car, takes her away and throws her into the hell she thought she'd left in the slums and mountains of Burma.

She never ever mentioned these nightmare scenarios to Kit. Though scary, they were born of silly, baseless paranoia. She let each scenario play itself out, knowing that in the end Kit's strong hand would reach in to solve the problem.

That, especially, she never let him know.

She sucked the sweat from one of his longest fingers and said, "What about seers? Psychics? Can they know what's going to happen?"

"Edgar thinks he can. He sees glorious fortunes showering down upon him."

"Oh, really? And how's that going to happen?"

"Gumballs."

"Gumballs?"

"Tons and tons of gumballs. He's going to be the Amazonian

King of Gumballs. I swear. That's his plan."

"Oh, he has a plan, does he?"

"Chewing gum far and wide. He's going to install these big fancy dispensers all over Amazonia. According to him, he's bringing civilization to the Stone Age. He says he wouldn't be surprised if someday they put up a statue of him."

"Yeah, right. And who's going to chew this gum? Monkeys? Jaguars? Toucans?" Ysa's mind treated her to an image of jungle animals blowing blue, red, yellow and green bubbles as they swung from trees and stalked the jungle floor. She imagined a children's book.

"There's a lot of people living in the rain forest," Kit said. "You'd be surprised." He was quoting Edgar almost word-for-word. "There's Indians, gold miners, loggers, farmers, hunters, little villages, even some towns with ten to twenty thousand people."

"Oh, yeah? Name one. Besides Manaus."

Manaus she already knew. It was the only city of any size upstream from Belém. But she'd never heard of anywhere else. She tried to distract him by scratching the blonde fuzz at the top of his left thigh.

"OK," Kit said. "How about Itaituba."

"What kind of tuba?" She could tell he wasn't entirely focused on the city with the funny name. His scrotum was roiling with desire.

"Itaituba," he gasped as if it were suddenly irrelevant. "It's half...halfway up the Tapajós. Keep doing that."

"Hey, you really know your geography, don't you?" She was studying the geography of his groin, the mountains and valleys that were moving around like something in a slow earthquake. She was crazy about Kit. She couldn't keep her hands off him. She wouldn't let him talk geography for long. But he held out long enough to mention Jacaréacanga.

"Zhaca-what?" she said, wondering how he knew so much after three days in Brazil.

"Jacaréacanga. It's way upstream from Itaituba, which is already plenty upstream from the Amazon at a point which is way upstream from here."

Ysa pulled back from Kit's swelling desire. She smelled trouble. "What's that place got to do with us?"

"Well, it isn't us. It's mostly Edgar. He's got this plan to install gumball machines in all the places where there's nothing else. Jacaréacanga is just the jumping off place. That's as far as civilization goes. He's going to put one machine there and then branch out. Every Indian village is going to have one. Every gold mine. Every logging camp. Every little school and military outpost. Everybody gets a gumball machine."

"Wait a minute. Go back to the part about it's *mostly* Edgar."

Kit's strong broad hand cupped her shoulder blade and pulled her up to lie atop him. She loved to ride his chest as it swelled and sank, pressing to her breast and pulling back. In sleep, his heart beat six times between each exhalation, the slow *k-thub...k-thub...k-thub* of a healthy man at rest. He loved to stroke her silky yellow hair as she lay on he pillow of his chest. When he spoke, she could hear the words forming deep within him.

"Well," he said. "It is Edgar. But he's invited us to go with him."

Ysa raised her head to look him in the eye. "To that place?"

"Repeat after me: Jacaréacanga."

"Zhaca-reh-a-kanga. How do you spell it?"

He told her. She peeled her sweaty skin from his and grabbed Edgar's big green-and-yellow English-Portuguese dictionary from a shelf. With her elbows on Kit's chest, her breasts lightly against him, she searched the pages until she found half the word. *Jacaré*.

"Alligator," she reported.

"I like this place already. Look up the other half of the word. *Canga*."

Adjusting herself to keep her elbows from digging into her one and only, she flipped back through the dictionary, looking for the C's.

"*Canga*," she said. "Yoke."

"Yolk like egg yolk?"

"No, dummy, yoke for an oxen."

"Alligator Yoke. I love it. Let's let Edgar take us to Alligator Yoke."

That place sounded perfect – the frontier of civilization, the outskirts of the twentieth century. Exactly what she was looking for. Ysa dropped the dictionary and told Kit she loved him. He pressed his open mouth to her head, squeezed her hair in both hands, searched out her ear and breathed into it. Her sweat turned to ice in a wave that swept over her body, head to toes. He was strong and hard and ready. She arched against him and brought him inside, turning her belly to lava. He took her breast in his mouth, toyed with the nipple, sucked it to full height. She rose and descended, rose and descended, extracting his passion and filling herself with it. Then they fell back to the damp sheets and bathed in the caress of the overhead fan.

Yes, she would go to Alligator Yoke with Kit. She would go anywhere with him. But she worried about Soong Tan.

"Is it a place for an eleven-year-old?" she asked, quite out of the blue.

Kit knew what she meant. He said, "Hey, it isn't a war zone, you know? It's a town. People live there. Kids. I wouldn't want Soong to live in a place called Alligator Yoke, but hell, how bad can it be to visit?"

Ysa felt better. She trusted Kit. He could do anything. What could possibly go wrong?

Chapter Three

The Gumball Gods

The boat had rats. Elizama knew that before they arrived at the dock. She, Ysa, Kit and Soong Tan were still squashed up against each other in the back and front seats of a Volkswagen cab. The driver had the air conditioning on, but it did little good. It was a cab full of clam chowder.

Elizama hadn't actually seen these rats or even the boat they called home. She saw them in her head, a vision. "Kilo-rats," she called them.

Ysa almost threw up just thinking about a rat the size of a football.

But Edgar said, "Don't worry about it. They're down in the hold, with the bananas or whatever."

"No bananas," Elizama injected. "Bananas come down ze heever. We go up ze heever."

"What goes up the river?" Ysa asked, trying to eclipse the image of fat rats. "What products?"

"Oh, everysing ze peoples need. Oil for coo-king. Kerosene.

Cigahettes. Cachaça. Everysing."

"And recreational multichewable coin-operated snack food dispensers," Kit added. "Can't leave without the recreational multichewable snack food dispensers."

"Is going to make much money," Elizama said, rubbing her palms together. When she smiled, her teeth looked big and white behind her bright red lips. Ysa thought she looked like the kind of woman who could make the most of a big pile of money. She looked like the shopping type, and from what Ysa had seen so far, she had little on her mind besides acquisition. Much of what she had acquired she was taking on her trip up the Amazon. It was in a footlocker in a taxi following behind them. Ysa could imagine the clothes therein – brilliant red Bermudas, filmy peasant blouses, T-shirts with things written in English, eighty-seven pairs of shoes, forty pounds of make-up.

Ysa wasn't that type. She didn't need florescent lipstick to make men notice her. It didn't matter what she wore. On this trip, she wore a simple shift held up by spaghetti shoulder straps. It let air circulate around her body. Kit seemed to like it. He touched her a lot. When he touched her shoulder, his finger went under a shoulder strap. When he reached for her knee, his pinky would go up under the hem. Ysa liked that. Meanwhile, he was always joking around with Elizama, trying to learn Portuguese, being a regular clown but not showing any kind of interest in her. Not that Ysa was worried. But she had her eye on him.

She had to. He was too close to perfect. Smart and loving and responsible and better looking than any normal person. Every girl in the world wants a man like that.

The taxi took them down to a dock on the river and pulled up at a boat that looked like it most certainly had rats. Kilo-rats. It seemed to lean up against the dock as if exhausted, arthritic, maybe a little drunk. A bunch of guys in nothing but little shorts were loading boxes and gunny sacks into the hold on the lower deck, which was only about a foot above the water. The men were dark, sweaty and muscular.

Ysa whispered, "They look like slaves."

"Zey are," Elizama said. "Zey work for food and cachaça and somesing like tree reais a day. Is nossing."

"But they look like they're having fun."

"Zey are. Zat's what ze cachaça's for. You give zem a little wiss lunch and zey sink zey are in heaven."

Cachaça had the same effect on Ysa, though she didn't drink it with lunch. It was made from distilled sugar cane juice and had a kick like a mule. But, as Kit said, what's wrong with getting kicked by a mule once in a while?

Kit wasn't worried about the dock workers. He was worried about the boat. It was made of wood and needed painting, which to him meant the wood had to be at least a little rotten, which might be OK in some places but not in a river famous for its piranha and electric eels. It had three decks: one down near the water for the cargo, a middle deck that was open on the sides, and an upper deck, really just a roof over the middle deck. Kit thought it looked like the kind of vessel you hear about sinking in thirty seconds flat in the middle of a school of piranha and alligators. But he didn't say anything. He just made plans for evacuation. As soon as he reached the end of the gangplank, he knew where the life preservers and fire extinguishers were.

Edgar wasn't worried about the boat. He was worried about his gumball machines. Only after a lot of asking around did he find out they'd already been put on board and stored down in the hold. Which made Edgar go berserk.

"Não," he told some guy on the dock. "Não fucking way. Elizama...explain to this guy..." Edgar spoke medium-advanced Portuguese, but when something really important needed saying, he called in Elizama. The really important thing in this case was that the gumball machines absolutely could not be down in the hold with the rats.

"Rats love bubble gum," he told Kit and Ysa while Elizama rattled off about ten thousand words that somehow added up to mean não fucking way. "We already learned that the hard way. Down at the bus station. They chewed right through the plastic and climbed up into the storage ball. They ate so much gum they died in there. Their guts busted open. Not that that gave me any satisfaction. I still had to replace half the stock."

"Half?" Kit blurted. "The gum was in there with dead rats and you didn't replace it?"

"Hey," Edgar said, leaning in close and shifting to a whisper. "These people don't care. Especially if they don't know. Did you know they still have elephantiasis in this town? Elephantiasis."

"They probably got it from the goddam gum."

Edgar liked that one. He guffawed through his big, toothy grin and smacked Kit on the back. "You kill me, bro," he said. "You really slay me."

Elizama reported. The guy on the dock could do nothing. It

wasn't his job. It wasn't his boat. They'd have to go talk with the captain.

So they boarded the boat, the 21 de Março – the 21st of March. Ysa said it reminded her of an old Mississippi steamboat, sort of, except smaller and with a pointed bow and no paddle wheel or smokestacks or steam, but it was made of wood and looked like it could burst into flames at any moment. They found the captain down in the hold, swinging in a hammock, smoking a cigarette, reeking of cachaça. He was wearing a tie-dye T-shirt over his rotund beer-belly, green plaid shorts over his spindly legs, black knee socks slung low around his ankles, and no shoes on his feet. He looked Elizama up and down as she explained the problem with the gumball machines and the rats and the importance of sanitation. When she finally finished her impassioned plea, the captain tilted his head toward Edgar and said, "You are married to him?" Ysa didn't understand until the man indicated his own wedding band.

Elizama confessed that she was indeed married to Edgar. That shifted the captain's sleazy gaze to Ysa. He looked her up and down but then saw Kit's hard, cold look and came back to Elizama. "OK," he said as if he already knew he'd regret letting these gringos onto the 21st of March. "Move your damned gumball machines. Put them up on the leisure deck. But don't ask my crew to do it."

So Edgar and Elizama returned to the dock to negotiate with the workers. Kit and Ysa stayed to string up their hammocks on the passenger deck. That's how you travel on these boats. In hammocks. That's your cabin: a hammock. You want to sit down somewhere, you sit in your hammock. You want to sleep, you sleep in your hammock. You want to change your clothes, you pull your hammock up around you and do it in there. You want to make love, well, you wait till the lights are out and then you do it quietly while you sway in the breeze. Ysa summed it up rather well in a postcard to Susan. She wrote, "A Carnival Cruise it ain't."

At first she liked it. They set up their five hammocks like covered wagons in a circle, with all their baggage in the middle. They were all swinging in the breeze and thinking about lunch while Edgar hustled a crew of slave-types from the hold to the roof with twelve gumball machines, two men to each machine, twelve trips up and down. Edgar, nervous as an old maid watching gorillas handle her priceless china, had to supervise each twist and turn up the narrow ladders and through hatches barely wide enough. As each one came up onto the passenger deck, Edgar couldn't resist showing it off to the passengers. Each machine was a different model. One had the siren and pinwheel. One had little stairs going down instead of a spiral chute. One had stairs and a chute. One had a computer chip that said, "*Muito obrigado, amigo!*" – "Thanks a lot, friend!" Another one said, "*Compra mais uma!*" – Buy one more! All this in Edgar's voice, no less. The passengers marveled at the machines. Unfortunately ,nobody had money for gum. Most of them didn't have money for shoes.

Topside, Edgar had all the machines huddled together under a plastic tarp and bound with a rope so they wouldn't fall over. They looked like a bizarre Mardi Gras football team seeking shelter from the elements. When he finally joined his family at their hammocks, he went straight for a bottle of cachaça in his trunk. "I need this," he said, lying back to pour it straight into his mouth from several inches above. "I deserve this."

Elizama said, "Tcht," and turned her head to face away from him. "I hope you don't be drunk all zeh way to Itaituba."

"Not me," he said. "Maybe close to it, but not drunk."

Much to Ysa's surprise, Kit said, "Lemme try some of that." He took the bottle, leaned back in his hammock and poured a trickle right into his mouth the same way Edgar had done. He grimaced but said, "Cachaça and I could develop a relationship."

Ysa said, "You better not." She was surprised to hear herself saying it. Kit didn't drink a lot, and she never gave him any problem about it. As a matter of fact, she drank more than he did. But she had a woman's instinct about a man taking a little too much pleasure from a bottle, even for a second. It's a bad sign.

The boat finally got underway. It just kind of chugged along, hugging the coast. That's what Ysa called it. The coast. Because the river's so wide that sometimes you can't see the other side. For the first day it didn't matter that it wasn't a Carnival Cruise. They were just swinging in their hammocks and watching the jungle go by. Ysa had little binoculars so she could watch for animals. Elizama never stopped talking except when Edgar interrupted her.

Soong Tan was all over the boat, friends with passengers and crew alike. Ysa tried to get her to stay out of the hold, which she pictured as crawling with kilo-rats. But there was no stopping her. She was already speaking a funny little Portuguese crossed with English and Burmese. Kit kept quiet and took the occasional swig of cachaça.

But then Ysa discovered the bathroom. Three toilets for fifty passengers, most of whom weren't especially well potty-trained. Three showers, too. Ysa said the floors were so slimy she had to wear sandals or catch instant gangrene. The water was just river water. No hot. No cold. Just the temperature of the day.

Not that lukewarm was going to kill anybody on a hot tropical afternoon, but I think maybe Ysa was expecting just a little more comfort on her Amazon vacation. As for the leisure deck, the "leisure" part consisted of some benches you could sit on for as long as you could stand the sun. Benches and all the gumballs you could eat.

Edgar spent his time making enemies at the dining table that stretched across one end of the passenger deck. When it wasn't being used for a meal, men played dominoes there. Of course Edgar cleaned up. Not that the pennies of peasants amounted to much, but he took great satisfaction in scooping them in. They tried to win back their hard-earned pittances in poker, but again Edgar's game skills out-shined them all. He came back to the circle of hammocks patting a jingly little bulge in his pocket.

"They should have bought gum," he said with a big smile. " I gave them a chance. At least they'd have something to show for their money."

"Why don't you treat them to a round of gum, Edgar?" Ysa suggested. "Let everybody have a piece. Show off your machines. What the heck. It's their money."

Edgar tipped another squirt of cachaça into his maw, wiped himself off with his bare forearm, and tilted his head in consideration.

"Let's do it," Kit said, swinging around in his hammock. "Gumball kings, hell. Let's be gumball gods. Hey, gimme a snorta that stuff."

Edgar passed the bottle. Ysa gave him a look. He looked back, then took a quick hit. "Come on, Ed," he said, still looking at Ysa. "Let's go buy us some gumballs for the gang."

Good thing they went, too. Drunk or not – the jury's still out on that one – they didn't need a whole heck of a lot of brains to figure one thing out: their gumballs were melting in the hot tropical sun.

Not completely melting. They hadn't turned into tutti-frutti lava or anything. But they were all stuck together. Edgar loosened them by banging his fist on the plastic globe, but it was obvious they were going to have big gumball problems well before they got to Itaituba.

"We've got to get these things out of the sun," Edgar said.

"What an emergency!" Kit shouted to the broad equatorial sky.

"Trouble is, who's going to do it?"

"Never any slaves around when you need them."

"Maybe I can get some of those peasants to help me," Edgar said. "We're all friends."

Kit said nothing. He didn't expect much, and that's exactly what Edgar got. He lobbied all over the passenger deck, pulling on guys and saying, "*Vamos! Vamos!*" But they wanted nothing to do with him. Not after he'd taken their miserable excuses for life savings. He came back up to the leisure deck, wiped sweat from his eyes and said, "Looks like it's you and me, buddy."

"This is not a problem for a couple of gumball gods like us." Kit always liked a challenge, and he got bored much too easily. Moving twelve giant gumball machines down two decks looked a hell of a lot more interesting than hanging around in a hammock. He embraced one machine like a sumo wrestler, leaned back and lifted the thing an inch off the deck.

"How many gumball you got in these things, Ed?" he grunted.

"Two thousand, each one. It's the motor that weighs so much. That and the car battery."

Kit ended up dragging the thing across the deck to the ladder that led to the passenger deck. "You better get down there and support it from below," he said.

So Edgar went down first. Elizama came over to coach. "Be carefully," she said, her fists gripped tight.

Ysa said, "I think you'd be better off just letting them melt," but nobody was listening. Edgar shouted, "OK! Ease 'er down onto my shoulder." But that didn't work at all. The weight tilted him back. He lost his grip on the handrail and then on the stairs of the ladder, and then the gumball machine descended upon him, bouncing down the little stairs like a demon out of Disneyland. Edgar fell flat but rolled to the side just as the machine dived headlong to the deck. The plastic globe shattered like Christmas ornament, and two thousand gumballs clattered across the middle deck of the 21st of March, dodging around the baggage, scurrying under the hammocks, rumbling past the dining table, diving over the side like lemmings blipping into the dirty brown water of the Amazon.

Chapter Four

Love in a Muted Womb

Things went downhill after that. Distressed at his busted recreational multichewable coin-operated snack food dispenser, Edgar slipped into morose depression. He lay in his hammock, hugging a pillow, staring at nothing. Kit, always the responsible one, used the power of the almighty dollar to persuade a couple of crew members to help him move the machines down to the hold. The machines, too, looked depressed, leaned up against each other in a dark area behind at least a thousand plastic cases of bottled beer.

"Rat bait," Kit told Ysa at the dining table.

"Do you think I care?" She reached across the table to help herself to a ladle of spicy fish stew. It was very heavy on the coriander and some herbs she had never tasted before. Twelve other passengers sat with them and Soong Tan. Three dozen others waited their turn. Those seated served themselves from three tureens. They were jolly folks, laughing and talking even though they hadn't met until the day before. Their dining behavior was both polite and crude. Before taking their first bite, they would make a symbolic gesture with their bowls to offer food to anyone who hadn't eaten. They spoke those magic words, *por favor* and *obrigado*. But they kept their elbows on the table and leaned in low to the bowls and slurped from their spoons and smacked their lips as they carefully plucked meat from the long, thin fish bones.

"Sweetness," Kit said, secretly touching her bare knee below the table. "Don't blame me."

"He's your brother. Soong Tan, chew with your mouth closed, please."

"He's only sort of my brother, and this gumball business is his business. We're just going along for the ride. Remember?"

"Tcht."

She obviously wasn't enjoying the ride. Kit felt a little guilty but not real guilty. She was the one who wanted to see the Amazon. If she'd wanted to see it from the deck of a luxury liner, well, she should have said so.

Elizama wasn't having such a good ride, either. She didn't like seeing one of her gumball machines bite the dust before it had sold a single ball of gum. Nor could she suffer the destruction of a machine and loss of two thousand gumballs in silence. Standing over Edgar's hammock, she berated him in words visibly ferocious. Ysa, just a few feet away in her hammock, understood only a few of the words, including *estúpido* and *idiota*, which were repeated several times and punctuated with the longest, nastiest, sharpest index finger she had ever seen. Some of the other words could have been applied to the 21st of March bathroom just as well as they applied to

Edgar. Everybody else on board understood everything, and Ysa understood their smirks well enough. The herd of gumballs that had escaped into the river would probably go down in Amazon history, becoming part of the lore of the river that would be passed down through many generations to come.

Soong Tan, running around in little yellow clip-clop sandals, mashed her big toe on something in the hold. When she first rose up through the hatch and came across the deck limping and bleeding – but not crying – Ysa's first thought was that she'd been bitten by a rat. But no, she'd whacked it up against an anchor or something.

That's when Ysa discovered that the hydrogen peroxide in her medical kit had spilled, probably because some irresponsible drunkard had been pawing through there in search of aspirin or something. If she needed disinfectant, she'd have to find it herself. God only knew what filthy, rusty, contaminated iron thing her foot had found down there in kilo-rat country. The obvious thing to do was go see the captain, which was going to call for some Portuguese. Elizama was asleep. Ysa thought it best to leave her that way. She could figure something out for herself.

So she and Soong Tan limped on up to the little cabin where the captain stood at his big, round wooden wheel. With his wide belly perched atop his short, stilt-like legs, he looked like an over-grown misshapen elf from out of the tropical woods. Ysa knocked gingerly on the side of the open door and said, "*Pardón, senhor capitão...ummm*" He took his eyes from the river for only two seconds. He spent the first second eating Ysa's face, the next second ravishing her body in a downward motion, the third second grasping the basic situation of the toe that she was pointing to. With a nod, he turned his attention right back to the river. After a slight alteration in course, he called out for someone named Rogério. Rogério popped in and took the wheel. The *capitão* took Ysa and Soong Tan to his cabin just behind the wheelhouse.

And closed the door behind them.

Oh, he had a first aid kit, all right. He gave it to Ysa and patted a spot on his little bed where she could sit to perform her little operation. She couldn't very well just walk out. Soong Tan was standing there breathing hard, her big toe, all bloody, sticking straight up in the air. So Ysa sat and had Song Tan sit next to her, turned sideways so her foot was in Ysa's lap. The captain sat down, too.

Real close. His thigh and hip against hers. His big belly all but in her lap. He made cooing noises and examined the toe very closely. His arm came around behind Ysa as if to hold her steady. Ysa just wanted to finish the job as quickly as possible and dash out of there. But just as she had one hand on Soong Tan's quivering foot and the other on a ball of cotton dripping wet with peroxide, the captain leaned over for a little nibble of her neck. She tried to shrug him off, but he stay in there, his tongue licking out to touch her skin like a hot garden slug. A nauseating stench of stale cachaça, sweat and cigarettes oozed out of him. His whiskery cheek scraped her neck like rough sandpaper.

Ysa wasn't one to put up with that stuff. If the *capitão* had known what she'd done to the drug lord of Burma, he wouldn't have been pushing himself on her. But he didn't know, and she was stuck with Soong Tan's throbbing foot in her lap and the hydrogen peroxide ready to go. It wasn't the right moment to dismantle the man. So, good nurse that she was, she pretended nothing was going on. She gently dabbed the disinfectant onto the toe while Soong Tan winced and sucked in air and the good *capitão* accepted the lack of resistance as evidence of desire. He went for her ear, first nuzzling it with his nose, then kissing it, then probing it with his tongue.

Normally, once a man's got his tongue in Ysa's ear, she's pretty much his. What happens after that is pretty much out of her control. In this case, however, she felt most disgust, but it was mixed with just a teensy bit of desire.

Kit knew, too. So when he eased open the door just a bit, looking for his woman and little girl, he no doubt sized up the situation at first glance. Apparently the captain, his face buried under Ysa's sweet yellow hair, didn't even notice Kit's arrival. Ysa jabbed back with an elbow, but she had to do it lightly to keep from hurting Soong Tan. To Kit, it looked more like a nudge than a jab.

Kit said, "So, what's going on?"

That snapped the captain out of his desire. For a second, he looked scared. In Brazil, messing with another guy's wife is grounds for murder. But he quickly shifted that into a look of indignation. Kit read his face correctly. It said, What the hell are you doing in my cabin? Kit, not knowing Portuguese, came back at him with a look that said, What the hell are you doing with my woman and kid in your cabin? Ysa, smelling testosterone in the air, said, with typical cool, "Don't do anything till I'm done." And she continued to dab on the peroxide and examine Soong Tan's torn flesh. It didn't seem to need stitches.

Soong Tan shook her stinging foot and said, "Ooooooo, Ysaaaaa!"

"One second more. Then Kit can punch the nice captain in the nose."

The men continued to glare at one another. The captain said something Kit could not understand. Then Kit said something the captain could not understand. Ysa said, "*Momento...momento...*" and hurriedly wrapped a bandage around Soong Tan's toe.

"OK, gentlemen," she said, standing up. "Have at it." And she slipped out the room, Soong Tan in tow.

Kit could have pulverized the captain with his bare hands. He knew how to do that. And when Kit pulverizes somebody, they stay pulverized.

But Kit's not one to start a fight. Especially with the captain of the boat he's on. Kit's not dumb. Besides, he didn't really know what had been going on in the room before he showed up. Ysa hadn't exactly been fighting the guy off. So Kit did what he says is always best when you're faced with a fight. He turned around and walked away.

Ysa had expected more than that. She wanted some damage done. She really hated it when guys bothered her, which tended to happen a lot . You don't get yellow hair like that from a box. You have to get it from Norway and Holland. But what did it get her? Guys bothering her all the time.

For the rest of the day there wasn't a whole lot of talking around the gringo hammocks. Everybody was mad at everybody else. They all smelled like they needed showers. Only Soong Tan was happy. At Ysa's orders, she stayed within the circle of hammocks, keeping her foot clean by playing Crazy Eights with a couple of kids she'd met. She already knew enough Portuguese to explain the rules.

That night, as the passengers slept in their hammocks like fifty butterflies wrapped in colorful cocoons, Ysa awoke under the weight of a man. Without a word he slipped into the curved, muted womb of her hammock. She didn't even open her eyes. She knew who it was by his smell and the tongue that filled her ear like a warm animal burrowing into her head. She did not need to tell him to stroke her arms and then her belly and then up under her T-shirt to tease her nipples and gently rub her breasts in opposite directions. She did not need to tell him to put his mouth there. All she needed to do was keep quiet, to breathe without moaning, to try to keep the hammock from swinging too wildly as he kissed his way downward, across her ribs, across her tummy to the oasis of her navel. His tongue explored that fuzzy little cave as if it went so deep within her that he might find her soul in there. Indeed it felt as if he were extracting her soul through that little well of wet desire. Her fingers dug into his hair, moving his head in circles against her as she guided it places to where it felt really good. The hot, tropical air pulled sweat from every cell of her body and his, and her brain boiled over with steaming desire. Had she ever wanted him as much as now? She could not be blamed for what she did. Passion had taken control. It lifted her out of herself and left a throbbing body of flesh craving all the pleasure it could suck from any source it could find. Lifting her hips, she let his hands slide her panties down, inch by inch, his lips in hot pursuit. He nibbled at her thighs, inside and out. He slobbered over her knees, returned to her thighs, kissing spots he'd missed on the way down. His hands searched for curves and nooks and spaces which they desperately needed to visit. She wanted those hands and his lips in all those places, too. She wanted them everywhere at once. No sooner had he gotten her toes into his mouth than she wanted his head between her breasts, his fingers between her legs, his tongue in her mouth, his lips sliding down the small of her back, all at the same time, an impossibility of contortion. She could not have him or any one man that way, so she took what she got. And she loved it. She loved his weight upon her, inside her hot, tight hug of arms and legs. His animalistic thrusting rocked the hammock in a shuddering contrapuntal sway. She didn't care if anyone noticed the unusual movement of their private cocoon. She didn't care if the whole boat rolled over. All she wanted in that hour of overheated passion she was holding tight within her total embrace. So the next morning they were in love again. At least for a while.

Chapter Five

The Prediction

Soong Tan wrote Susan a letter.. Susan thought it was pretty funny how kids can be doing something while grown-ups think they're doing something else altogether. But for some reason Soong Tan thought she could tell somethings to Susan but not to Ysa.

Dear Susan,

You're a grown-up, more or less. Maybe you can tell me. How come the bigger people get, the more they sit around doing nothing? I don't get it. We're going up the Amazon on a boat. It's so cool! And all Ysa and Kit and the others do is hang out in the hammocks.

I'm already friends with a bunch of kids. We went down in the cargo hold. They knew their way around. We went crawling and climbing all around the cargo. There's this one spot where's there's a hole a bout big enough to stick your foot into if you wanted to, which you'd be stupid to do because if you wait long enough, pretty soon a big, fat rat comes out. The kids had a sling-shot. We used it to shoot Brazil nuts at the rat. The nuts came from a big sack that we cut a hole in the bottom of. Pretty soon there were nuts all over the place, and we never hit the rat.

The crew sleeps down there. One guy has a huge turtle in a gunny sack. I think he's smuggling it. When he showed me, he held one finger to his lips and whispered, "Contrabanda." I'm pretty sure that means contraband. I couldn't think how to ask him why he was smuggling a turtle. I mean, I've heard of smuggling drugs, and I think I've heard of smuggling weapons, but smuggling turtles, that's a new one. I guess they smuggle different stuff here.

We're traveling with this weird lady named Elizama. She keeps making predictions. Everything predicts something for her. She can read your palm, read your tea leaves, read the dried coffee in the bottom of a cup. When a flock of big pink birds flew overhead, she gasped like she was dying and said, "Soong Tan, you be sure to stay close to Ysa!"

Like, how far does she think I'm going to get? Where does she think I'm going to go? I said, "What do you mean?"

"I see danger. I see you all alone wiss great danger all around. Many friends and great danger." Then she grabs my head with both hands and looks at me real close. She's got the grossest face, with bright red lips and blue stuff all around her eyes and her eyelashes plucked so she looks like a doll...an old doll with wrinkles a five o'clock shadow over her lip. She holds my head so close I can smell her lipstick and chewing gum. "You be carefully!" she says. "I do not know what weell hoppen, but you must be very, very carefully!"

Well, before too long I knew what she was talking about. I was down in the cargo hold playing hide-n-seek, which they call scondji-scondji here, and I was just running for home when I stubbed my toe on a piece of pipe that was lying there for no reason. Yow! That really hurt! It bled and everything. But at least because of it I got to see the captain's cabin, and you know what? You're going to think this is weird, so I'm kind of glad it happened. Now it's over with. Elizama warned me, and then it happened, and now I can forget about it. Thank God. Because the stuff she predicts, sometimes it comes true.

Yours truly,

Soong Tan

Chapter Six

The Bunnyhugger

Edgar snapped out of it in Santarém, where the Tapajós flows north into the Amazon. There they had to change boats, a pretty big deal when you've got a dozen gumball machines and the temperature's way over a hundred and you've got a medium-sized crowd watching because you're the most interesting thing to come up the river in two hundred years. According to Edgar, this was the arrival of civilization, He'd figured out he could buy a new storage globe to replace the one that had broken. It wasn't the end of the world.

They had to spend all day in Santarém waiting for a boat up the Tapajós. Crack entrepreneur that he was, Edgar saw it as opportunity. He deployed his machines across the dock like a row of Beefeaters. Performing a shameless "Step-right-up-and-get-yourself-a-gumball" routine, pointing out the machines' features with some kind of pointer, he all but dragged people up to the face of temptation. He passed out twenty-five centavo pieces to get a few kids to try it. As the pinwheels spun and the sparks shot out, the crowd went nuts. The full splendor of civilization had arrived. And all it cost was the equivalent of a U.S. quarter.

Later, in a not-too-sleazy open-front sidewalk bar just across the street, Edgar counted his take. He had piles of coins all over this table, silvery columns among the sweaty glasses of beer. Soong Tan kept to her own table, where she worked on a postcard to her sixth-grade class at Beauville Elementary School. It said, "This place reminds me of Burma," she wrote, "but at least I'm not alone."

Ysa was scribbling away at a letter that already almost filled a notebook. She just kept jotting down her thoughts and observations. She thought that maybe if something exciting happened she'd write a book about it. So far, however, it was just rambling notes, a conversation with a friend who wasn't there to hear it.

His chin down at table level so he could see the little towers of his fortune, Edgar said, "Twenty-eight reais and twenty-five centavos in two hours." He nudged the columns around to make the money look like as much as possible. "Not bad."

Elizama took up her beer glass and rotated it to find a spot she had not yet stained with a curve of blood-red lipstick. The glass looked like it suffered from multiple lacerations. "What you can to buy wiff twenty-eight reais?" she asked in a cynical voice. She seemed to be thinking in terms of Mercedes Benzes.

"Fourteen bottles of Brahma beer," Edgar replied. He tapped one of the coins on the empty bottle. A waiter came to life and rushed over with another bottle.

"That's just two hours in one location," Edgar explained. "Now imagine twenty-four hours a day in twelve locations. You sure you don't want in on this, Kit?"

Ysa could tell that Kit was already tired of hearing about it. "I'll have to talk with my attorney," he said, gazing out over the river. It glimmered in the early-afternoon sun. Several buzzards soared in lazy circles, riding the heat while waiting for something dead to float by. "What happens if some kid chokes on a gumball way out in the jungle. Can I be held liable?"

"They don't have liability in this country," Edgar said, missing Kit's cynicism. "Responsibility is a foreign concept. Here comes more logs."

He pointed upstream at four barges stacked high with enormous trunks.

"I thought they stopped cutting down the rain forest," Ysa said.

"Ha! No way. They might talk about it, but as long as there's money in it, they'll keep cutting it down. It's entirely possible those logs came off a federal forest reserve. But they're worth so much that the loggers can afford to buy off the polícia militar."

This disgusted Ysa. She was a confirmed bunny-hugger. Save the salamanders. No nukes. Adopt a dolphin. All that stuff.

"Don't they ever worry about oxygen?" she asked.

"Not till oxygen's worth money," Edgar said. Something about the gleam in his eye, a laser trained on a small fortune in logs, told her that he didn't give a damn one way or the other.

Kit said, "Where's the gold? I thought there was gold in the Amazon." He was happy they were off the topic of gumballs. He had his shirt pulled up a bit so his belly could cool off. He had his shoes off, too, his feet up on one of the shaky steel chairs.

"We'll be up in gold territory," Edgar said. "I wouldn't recommend drinking any river water unless you know what's upstream. It's all poisoned with mercury."

"They have mercury mines?"

"No, dummy. They use it to mine gold. When they've got a little gold dust mixed in with sand and dirt, they stir in a little mercury. It combines with the gold. Then they pour it off and heat it up. The mercury evaporates and leaves the gold behind."

"That doesn't sound too healthy," Ysa said. "Mercury's highly toxic. I wouldn't want to breathe it in."

"Health isn't their concern. Gold's their concern. And don't you see how all this relates to gumballs?"

Kit smiled wryly. "I had a feeling it would."

Edgar continued. "When you come right down to it, what good's gold? It's worthless. You can't eat it, can't live in it, can't brush your teeth with it."

"So?"

"So suppose the nearest supermarket's three days away by canoe. Your boss is paying you big money to muck around in the mud, not to mention poison yourself with mercury. The only thing you've got to spend your money on is cachaça and bubble gum. You're bored and you've got a hangover. So what do you do?"

Kit thought a second and said, "Any girls around?"

Ysa gave him a playful shove with her elbow. Edgar said, "Sure. Plenty of girls. And they've got every disease under the sun. And there stands a magnificent, disease-free gumball machine."

Kit was tired of this. Very, very tired. The heat hung over him like a heavy wool blanket. "I'd buy gum," he said. "I'd buy the goddam gum. OK?"

"My point exactly."

Kit surrendered in silence. Nobody said anything. They just sat, oppressed with the humidity, looking through the heat waves rippling off the street, vaguely seeing the gumball machines lined up on the dock, the little blue and white boat that they would soon board, the tan river beyond that, and the vast blue sky bleached pale from the sun. Ysa wanted nothing more than to climb into her hammock and doze off her beer-soaked doldrums as a light water-breeze drifted across the deck. She was tired of the Amazon. In fact, she hadn't even seen jungle yet. No monkeys. No anacondas. No jaguars or toucans or peccaries. Just an endless parade of medium-sized trees along the bank, second-growth forest replacing a jungle long ago cut down or burned. The upper Tapajós was supposed to be primal forest, but by this point, she really didn't care. She was hot, tired, sweaty, dirty, and her bowels felt and sounded like trouble brewing. At this point she was pushing on for Soong Tan's education and Kit McCracken's entertainment. She herself had had enough.

Due to lack of absolutely anything else to do, and to kind of pay rent at the table, and at Edgar's relentless insistence, they went ahead and had another beer. Soong Tan had another soda, some Brazilian stuff called *guaraná*. Everybody was just starting to think about the possibility of finally raising their overcooked carcasses and hauling them across the street to the boat when a couple of hippy-types came along.

Not hippies, exactly, but youngish, early twenties, she in a long flowery dress of translucent fabric, he in stylishly torn and faded jeans, both of them with backpacks, both pulling cardboard boxes on little luggage carts, both wearing sandals, both looking just as hot and sweaty as the other. Her ditch-water brown hair hung in a ponytail almost to her waist. His did, too, though it was blonde and prettier than hers. They'd come upon the bar by apparent accident, suddenly looking up and in, then saw Edgar's morose band of gumball hucksters. Their reaction was that of all gringos when they meet some of their species in a way-off place. They noticed and tried to pretend they didn't. But they couldn't. There was no denying it. They were all from the same place. The first words from the girl's mouth were crisply British: "Oh!" she chirped. "Gringos...right?"

The first thing Kit noticed about her was her light blue eyes. They sparkled. As he would later tell Ysa, they had absolutely no effect on him what-so-ever. It was just something he happened to notice.

To which Ysa would say, "Yeah, right."

The first thing Ysa noticed, of course, was that the girl had a large bead of sweat dangling from a single curly whisker on the end of her chin. And the guy, she said, looked like he hadn't shaved in about two days. Blonde beard.

She just happened to notice.

So there they were, everybody just happening to notice everybody else, and the girl's question was hanging in the air like wet laundry. *Gringos, right?*

Kit finally said, in clipped British, "Right...gringos."

"Whew," the girl said, and she stripped off her pack. It almost threw her off balance. The guy remained standing, his thumbs under the straps of his pack as if he expected to move on in the next thirty seconds. Ysa looked mildly miffed. Kit swung around a chair from a neighboring table.

"Have a seat," he said. "You look bushed."

Ysa said, "We were just leaving."

"Ve are lookink for a boat," the guy said. He had a German accent. "You haff heard off it?"

"Heard of it," Edgar blurted. "We've practically bought it. That's her right across the street. The one with the gumball machines on the...roof! Goddammit, I told them..."

"You're kidding," the girl says. She was one of those chicks who's just sooooo gushy about everything? "You're kidding," she gushed. "Are you going to...to...what's that place, Goose?"

"Jacaréacanga." With his German accent he made it sound like Transylvania or something. Ysa's skin crept. Two degrees south of the equator and she feels the chill of goose flesh. Maybe it was because he was wearing a little necklace of what looked like snake fangs. Behind her, Soong Tan slurped the last of her *guaraná* and said, "I'm still waiting for somebody to spell that place for me."

"Yeah, that place," the chick says.

"We sure are," Edgar said, taking control by reaching out his hand. "Edgar Entwhistle," he said. The girl shook it. Her name was Gaia. The guy was Goose, short for Gustav. He took off his pack before shaking everybody's hand.

"So," said Kit. "What's going on in Jacaréacanga?"

Gaia did all the talking. Ysa knew right then and there that Goose had to be the brains of the outfit. Gaia was the energy. She spoke at the speed of sound, her train of thought a discombobulated torrent on no particular track. In a nutshell, she was out to save the world. Step one: toss a thousand tiny purple porpoises out of an airplane over a logging camp a hundred miles south of Jacaréacanga. She extracted a porpoise from her cardboard box. It was wrapped up in a tiny green parachute.

Ysa said, "I don't get it."

'It's a statement," Gaia said, raising her chin in a gesture of defiance. "Clear-cutting the jungle doesn't just hurt the local ecosystem. It reaches into the sea and around the world."

"But aren't they plastic?" Edgar asked. "Suppose one floated downstream and a porpoise choked on it?"

"Don't mind him,." Kit injected. "Have some beer." He handed her his glass.

"They aren't plastic. They're pressed bicarbonate of soda and soy solids, with grape juice added for coloring. It dissolves in water." She handed Edgar the little porpoise, freeing her hand for Kit's beer. "You could actually eat it."

So Edgar bit off the tail. It was kind of gummy and stuck to the front of his teeth. "Weird," he said.

"It iss psychology," Goose said in a serious growl. "If ve convince vun logger zat he does wrong, ve sink he vill convince uzzers."

Edgar, using his fingernail to peel purple bicarbonate of soda and soy solids off his teeth, said, "Good luck's all I got to say to that." His lips buzzed as he struggled to spit out a fleck of porpoise.

"Ve shoot get tickets for ze boat," Goose said to Gaia.

Too exhausted to move, she waved faintly in the direction of the dock. "You do it," she said. "I'll watch the stuff."

Goose obeyed, scuffing across the street to the dock and the boat. Kit signaled the waiter for another beer.

Elizama looked oddly suspicious as she reached across the table toward Gaia. "Please," she said. "Let me to see your hand."

Gaia extended it to the center of the table. Elizama turned it over, perused the palm, traced a few lines. "I'm going to live a long time," Gaia said. "I already know that." She was squinting into the sun, watching her Goose negotiate with someone at the boat.

"Zat's not what it says here," Elizama cooed sweetly. "It says somesing very strange. It says you will get lost and you will divide in two pieces. I sink zat means you will die, but I don't know."

"Let me see that hand." Gaia snatched it back to herself and held it up close to her face. She picked at it, then spit on it and rubbed a clean spot. "You know what it is?" she concluded. "I'm a Gemini. That's all."

Elizama looked dubious. "Maybe is," she said. "Maybe is not."

Ysa became conscious of her own heartbeat. It was an odd sort of fear. She thought it might be sunstroke or something. She didn't tell anybody, though, and she forgot about it when Elizama suddenly said, "I feel a storm coming on."

The sky was blue for as far as anybody could see, but Kit took advantage of the break in subject. He dragged his feet off the chair, slapped both knees and said, "Then we'd better get our gumballs in gear." He stood up and held his hand out over the sidewalk as if it might catch a drop of rain from the clear, blue sky. "You mean like a thunderstorm?" he asked.

Elizama tilted her head to the left. "Yes," she said heavily, "and no. Yes, like a sunderstorm, but no...not a sunderstorm. Somesing worse."

Chapter Seven

Alligator Yoke

Ysa didn't especially like the trip up to Jacaréacanga. It took another five days on two more boats. She spent the whole time writing an eighty-three-page letter, noting every little detail that crossed her mind. She explained how Soong Tan just loafed around because there were no kids on these boats. They carried only a few passengers, peasants who hauled their belongings in bundles and jugs. The first boat was a smaller version of the one that had come up from Belém. Ysa described the beer belly of a man in a nearby hammock and how he scratched it with great pleasure. She described the Tapajós, its clear water, its steep, forested banks, its emptiness of anything but the occasional canoe. The river gradually narrowed, from a couple miles wide where it joined the muddy Amazon, to only half a mile wide at Itaituba. In Itaituba, they had to get out to change boats. Because of a wall of rapids that stretched all the way across the river, they had to board the back of a cargo truck – gumball machines and all – and take a laborious three-hour ride up a dirt road to a backwater port where smaller boats stopped. There they boarded a motorized fuel barge, a craft not meant for passengers, but Edgar knew the owner of the fuel company, so they were able to hitch a ride. They strung their hammocks on a half-open deck stacked high with crates of basic necessities bound for Jacaréacanga. Below them rode ninety thousand liters of diesel fuel.

Ysa was scared to death Soong Tan would fall overboard without anyone noticing. The river was different above Itaituba, shallower and silently turbulent. The water swirled and bubbled and humped up over unseen boulders on the river bed. She saw whirlpools and imagined the little girl spinning around, arms upraised until she disappeared in the dark vortex. Amazonia was getting interesting, but she wasn't sure if she was glad. It was starting to look dangerous.

The vegetation on the bank, often just a short stone's throw away, became real rain forest, an uncut jungle of trees so high they seemed to dangle from the sky. She never saw any jungle animals, only birds. But at night, when they tied the barge to a tree, she heard them in there – screeches, gnawing, a snort, a maniacal laugh. She wondered whether snakes could follow a rope from a tree to a barge. She supposed they could if they wanted. She supposed they could rise right up and slink into a hammock. You wouldn't even know if they did...until you rolled over.

She slept light. She listened to mosquitoes and wondered whether they carried malaria. She listened to Soong Tan breathe. She listened to Kit breathe. She listened to Edgar snore and Elizama whimper and moan in her dreams. She wondered whether clairvoyants had different kinds of dreams. She wondered whether Elizama really was clairvoyant and what kind of storm she had foreseen, the one worse than a thunderstorm. Did they have tornadoes in tropical rain forests? Ysa wondered a lot of things. Sleeplessness at the fringe of a jungle gives a person time for that – that and letters, which explains the ninety-two pages that arrived in Virginia in Susan's mailbox in an envelope postmarked Jacaréacanga and plastered with enough Brazilian stamps to cover everything but her address.

Their hippy friends didn't relate to each other much. Goose spent hours at a time up on the bow, his legs over the edge, his feet just inches from the frothing water. Gaia seemed to spend an inordinate amount of time with Kit. He didn't seem to mind much. They played a lot of dominoes on the little table where everyone ate their one-dish meals, five people at a time. Gaia just talked and talked and talked. Kit just listened and listened and listened. Ysa couldn't tell whether he looked bored or not, but now and then he cracked a joke, and Gaia practically collapsed with laughter. But when she lost at dominoes, she stomped off in a huff, pouted in her hammock until dinnertime, then bounded out in the cheeriest of moods.

Once, just to get some kind of reaction out of Kit, Ysa went to sit with Goose. As she gingerly took a seat at the edge of the bow, she noticed him noticing her legs. Her sunburn had baked to a luscious tan,which her safari shorts showed to great advantage. Goose noticed.

She pumped him for information about Gaia. It turns out they'd met at a Narcotics Anonymous meeting in London. Ysa didn't dare ask him precisely what had led them there, but Goose, after hesitating, said, "I can only tell you she vas...ve both vas...how you say in English, ' very, very fucked up.'"

"But then you stopped."

"Oh, ya! Ve had to. If ve did not, ve die for sure."

"And now everything's OK?"

Goose kept his eyes aimed at the river where it passed beneath them in a constant licking of froth from under the bow. "OK, I guess," he said. "I think Gaia still has some problems. She doesn't use anymore...no, no more. But she suffered, how you say, effects. You know?"

Ysa just nodded, hoping he'd tell more.

He did. "She needs lisium now," he said.

"Lithium?"

"Ya, lisium. And Prozac. But sometimes she stops. She sinks she doesn't need it. And then...ho-boy! Such problems she makes!"

"What kind of problems?"

"Oh...I can't say. It is hard to describe. She becomes very depressed. She becomes...I don't know...crazy. You know?"

She knew.

Kit knew, too.

"You can tell," Kit said as they snuggled in her hammock after the boat had tied up and everyone else had gone to sleep. "The flightiness, the sudden bursts of happiness and fascination, the appearance of disconnectedness with anything in reality that might hurt. Besides, she asked me if I thought they might sell lithium in Jacaréacanga."

"You mean she's like...running out of it?"

"I didn't ask, but that would be my guess."

"Then what?"

"Well, I guess that's her problem. And Goose's. I guess they'll dump their porpoises and head for home."

He held her as they talked. His arms wrapped around her from behind. From where they lay they could see the Southern Cross, not to mention a million other stars they'd never seen before. His hands gently, absently stroked her breasts. The back of her head lay against his shoulder. Finally she whispered, "Do you find her attractive?"

"Who? Gaia?" She felt his head shake behind her. "Nah. Too skinny. And nuts to boot." He nuzzled through her hair to her neck and gave it a little lick in a certain place. Despite the heat of the night, the moist touch of his tongue sent a shiver clear down to her right knee. She wanted that tongue, but there was no way to turn around in the hammock without creating a major disturbance and attracting the kind of attention she did not want.

She closed her eyes. She had never heard of a man complaining about a girl being too skinny. Kit was just saying that. She was sure of it. He wanted her to think he wasn't interested. That meant he was. The day had come. She'd known it would. He had grown used to her. Bored. Along came someone who laughed at his jokes and looked him in the eye and sat with her legs crossed like a man, and that was the end of him.

She pulled his hand harder to her breast, pressed her nipple into the center of it. His broad hand was so strong and comforting. Her finger found a plump vein that curled around his knuckles. She did not want to lose him or even to share him, not even for a minute. She did not blame him for looking the other way, at another woman. Men looked. They always had; they always would. And women would always try to attract those eyes. And sometimes they attracted more than the eyes. If that nitwit bitch Gaia had any such intentions, she was dogmeat. The only question was how best to handle it.

Or maybe it was just her imagination. Just because he found Gaia's company entertaining didn't mean he was going to hop into bed with her.

But men did that, and Ysa wasn't sure whether any of them, even Kit, was immune to the urgings of the groin. She knew she could trust him in every possible way except maybe that one. And she wanted him completely, without exceptions. If Gaia made the wrong move, she'd find herself in a can of Alpo. And if Kit drifted a little too far, well...she'd just reel him back in. He'd be sorry, and she'd tuck away his regret like money in the bank.

Ysa's first postcard from Jacaréacanga – a Washington, D.C. postcard that she found in the bottom of her backpack – said, "This place is definitely worth the trip if you're into suffering." She described it as looking a lot like an old town out west back when the streets were dirt and people rode around on horses and shot each other with revolvers. Such is Jacaréacanga, except that as soon as you ride out of town, you're in a jungle. And the gnats! Great, frantic clouds of tiny black flies pounced on the new visitors as if they hadn't eaten in weeks. There they was in the middle of a tropical forest and they had to wear long pants and long sleeves.

It turned out there were two hotels in town. A normal person wouldn't set foot in either place, but one of them had electricity, from its own generator. The other didn't. Kit wanted to stay in the one that didn't. He said it was more real. Edgar thought that was a good idea because it was cheaper, only $7.00 instead of $16.00 at the fancy place. But Elizama pointed out that the fancy place had an indoor bathrooms, albeit just a couple, for all the guests. The other place had just one bathroom, an outhouse several yards from the back door. Ysa voted on Elizama's side, which made it a tie. Soong Tan broke the tie, voting the way Ysa told her to. Goose and Gaia went to the other place.

Edgar immediately went out in search of the airport. Elizama stayed behind in a room full of gumball machines. She hardly had room to move around. Not that she wanted to move much. Like everyone else, she was exhausted. She turned on her ceiling fan and lay down half-naked on her bed.

Ysa wanted a shower before she did anything else. Kit followed her down the hall. They hadn't been really alone in almost two weeks. It was so tight inside the little shower room that they could barely close the door. It was hard to strip off their clothes, but they helped each other, and neither was in the mood for elbow room. She was kind of in a hurry. She wanted his shorts down and off. She wanted him rising in her hand. She liked to feel him coming to life. But Kit wanted it slowly. He liked to take her bra off little by little, kissing her as she came out of it. He liked to be down there as he slowly rolled her panties around her bottom, across her thighs, bit by bit exposing her to his leer and lick.

It was crowded, but they managed to get each others' clothes off and then bring their flesh together as the water rumbled out of the broad shower head that hung a good three feet above them. They soaked and kissed and fondled and reviewed all the places they hadn't touched for so many days. Ysa remembered how much she loved him. No other man could be so firm and gentle. He loved her whole body, and he ignored no part of it. They cupped her shoulders, then slid down her spine to wallow in the water that slid down the small of her back. They caressed the curves of her buns, traced the line of her crack, tickled the tops of her thighs.

"How long do you think we'll be here?" he asked, breaking off from a succulent kiss.

"I could stay all day." She took his breast into her mouth and massaged his nipple with her tongue. His hand came to the back of her head.

"I meant in Jacaréacanga," he said. "Edgar seems to think he's gong to find a home for those gumball machines in about three days."

"I'd be surprised if he finished by the end of next year. Have you got the soap?"

He handed her a green bar of Brazilian soap. She lathered up her hands and proceeded to cover him with filmy suds that smelled of cheap perfume. He stroked her arms as she worked her way from his neck, across his blonde-fuzz chest, down his hard, flat belly, around the massive passion at his groin. He loved it when she stroked him there. He came to full, breathless, quivering attention. She left him that way, sliding her sudsy hands around his waist to the rock-hard mounds of his rear.

He pulled her upward to bring her against him, smearing her body across his, eating at her mouth, licking the insides of her cheeks, wrestling with her tongue, needing her. She wondered if it would be like this if they ever got married.

He stopped before he exploded, pulling back just in time. Her chest was slick with his suds. "Do you think you speak enough Portuguese to get us out of here?" he asked, now sliding his hands around her breasts, sending his fingers skiing off their slopes. "I mean, if we had to." Her nipples loved the attention. They rose and pointed at him. They glowed with urgent desire. How did he know just how to treat them, how to twirl around them with his thumbs, to flick them with his fingers? It felt as if he had her womb in his two soapy hands.

She spoke just to keep herself from orgasm. She didn't want her legs to collapse onto the slimy floor. The drain below looked like it might harbor flesh-eating invertebrates. "I have no idea how we'd get out. Either we wait for the next fuel barge, whenever that is, or maybe there's a plane at the airport."

"Oh, yeah. I bet there's a 747 waiting for us right there at Gate 15. Scratch me right down here, would you?"

He scratched her, too. He knew all the spots. Nobody else in the world knew where those places were, let alone how to scratch them just right. She gasped with inexpressible pleasure as his hand burrowed between her legs from behind. As if he knew of some secret anatomical pathway, his tongue wiggled under her earlobe, completing a connection stimulated by his hand below. He was such a wonderful man, so caring, so eager, and he desired her so much.

She was attempting to shinny up him when the shower head started spitting and coughing. The water flow reduced to a trickle. They should have used those last drops to wash the soap from themselves, but they didn't. They were too busy.

Edgar comes back from the airport. He's all excited. He's found a plane that will fit a gumball machine. The pilot has agreed to take him to a certain gold mining operation about an hour away.

"It's perfect," he says, punching his fist into the palm of his other hand, his eyes gleaming with a mixture of greed and dream. "It's the biggest mining camp within five hundred miles. And they've got a runway. Something like three hundred and fifty men there. They're panning out twenty kilos of gold a month. Do you have any idea how many gumballs just one percent of that money represents?"

He was pacing around the little dining area of the hotel. Ysa, Kit, Elizama and Soong Tan sat around one of two long tables. That was the image that remained in Ysa's head later, her image of Amazonia before everything started happening: the bunch of them sitting around in the heat, sucking up beer as if their lives depended on it, and Soong Tan off to the side, drinking guaraná and writing letters to her class. "Greetings from Bug City," she wrote, and "This is as far as I go," and ""I am sick of bubble gum. Sick, sick, sick, sick, sick."

Ysa felt guilty sitting around like that, but to go outside in Jacaréacanga was to subject yourself to the blood-sucking gnats and an assault of sunlight. Besides, they'd seen all of Jacaréacanga. Seven minutes to walk to the other end of town, five to walk back. Along the way they saw exactly two cars that looked like they might run, two that definitely wouldn't, four horses, a dog that looked like it had just lain down in the street and died, a vulture just standing there looking at it, a dozen lizards and about as many people.

"No airplane," Elizama said without looking up from her fingernails. She was brushing on a lacquer to keep them from chipping. Ysa had suggested flying back to Belém instead of taking boats. But Elizama said, "No airplane.Forget about. I saw one airplane in my dream. It crash-ed. It crash-ed but was very strange. Eet deedn't heet ze ground."

"Oh, my!' Ysa gasped, perhaps too theatrically. She was just trying to veer the conversation away from Edgar. She was by this time quite sure Elizama was full of hogwash. "Was anybody hurt?"

"I don't know," Elizama said, wagging her head. "But when one airplane crashes, zat usually happens, no?"

Ysa told me she was actually kind of comforted to hear this prediction. Nothing else Elizama had predicted had actually come to pass, not even the alleged rats on the boat out of Belém. If she predicted a plane crash, then only one thing was certain: no plane would crash. Not that Ysa would have minded Edgar going down in flames.

On the other hand, maybe Elizama's latest prediction was only half-wrong. Maybe there would be a plane crash that actually hit the ground. In fact, the more Ysa thought about it, the more that made sense. A plane that crashed without hitting the ground wasn't much of a crash. What was it going to do, crash into a cloud?

Along came Goose and Gaia, all washed up and looking chipper. Gaia entered the room with an exuberant "Greetings, gringos!" She embraced Elizama with the silly kind of little hug-and-kiss women do in Brazil. They hug without really touching each other, and they kissed by putting their cheek near each other and making little kissy noises with their lips. It's the kind of hug and kiss that's good for women who hate each other, perfect for simultaneous stabs in the back.

And of course Kit and Edgar stood up to get theirs, too. In both cases it was more like a Russian hug, full-bodied, with warm poundings on the back and wet kisses to the cheek.

Ysa remained seated.

Soong Tan didn't notice anything amiss.

Goose shook everyone's hand in a rather formal European way, tilting at the waist, dipping the head slightly, shaking with only the slightest movement of the hand.

"So," Edgar said with a clap of his hands, "anybody for a game of Canasta?"

"Canasta!" Gaia spouted. "How quaint. No, sorry. We don't play."

"But ve haff mate progress on our mission," Goose said. "Ve already haff found a small plane zat can carry all uff our porpoises. Ve shall be taking off tomorrow."

"Not we exactly," Gaia said. "The plane can only hold one pilot, one passenger and twenty thousand porpoises. So I shall be going, and Goose shall maintain ground control."

At this moment, Ysa felt a secret and slightly guilty glee. Maybe Edgar's plane would crash. Maybe Gaia's plane would crash. Ideally they would crash into each other. She thought, maybe that's what Elizama meant. There would be a mid-air collision. By the time they reached the ground, the crashing part would be all over. Technically speaking, the prediction would be true.

It was a dumb and cruel thought, and she knew it. Or at least later on she thought she knew it. She never really hoped it. That's what she told Susan, blubbering with tears, over a radio-telephone that cost twelve dollars a minute to connect with the rest of the world. The crash wasn't her fault. It was all Kit's fault. And she felt so guilty about it she could die.

That was her last contact from Amazonia. Those were her last words. "I just want to die," she said, her voice dripping with tears. "I just want to die." At that point, however, death was not an option.

Chapter Eight

Kit Gone

Actually there was one more letter. She mailed it within hours before her phone call. It arrived two weeks later.

Dear Susan,

Something terrible has happened. It's worse than you can imagine. Far, far worse. I can barely write the words. I write them only because they hurt. I want them to hurt. I want them to kill me. Nothing hurts more than this. Here it is:

Kit ran off with another woman, and now it looks like he's dead.

Her, too, or so I hope. I hope she's rotting in hell. Her and her fucking porpoises.

Fucking Edgar is fucking useless. He doesn't even care. I don't even know where he is. Nobody does. He's not dead. He didn't crash. We know that much. He's still flying around with his goddam gumball machines. Like fucking Santa Claus bringing his goodies to every God-forsaken mining and logging camp in Amazonia.

I have to tell you what happened. It has to be in writing. Because I might not come back.

Passion in an Improper Place

There's this Indian who lives in town. He's from some tribe way, way out in the bush. He looks like a regular person. I mean, he's got those Indian eyes that look practically Chinese, and that straight, shiny-black hair, almost like Soong Tan's, and he's about as short as her, too. But he wears jeans and a T-shirt and sunglasses just like everybody else. He's a Munducuru, which, in case you happen to meet one walking down the street, is pronounced Moon-doo-roo-KOO. His name, in case you ever need to know, is Ronsh.

Yesterday morning Ronsh showed up at the hotel. He wanted to know if we wanted to take a canoe up a little tributary to some kind of beautiful waterfall. Of course I was all for it. Jacaréacanga gets mighty boring after about fifteen minutes. Kit was in bed, taking his third nap of the day. Soong Tan had nothing to do but read Brazilian comic books. So I said, "Come on, Kit, let's do it!"

But it's like he's on drugs or something. He just lolls around. He's like that sometimes. Unless there's something real interesting to do, he just isn't interested. If it were a beautiful waterfall surrounded by anti-tank missiles, he'd be all for it. Up and at 'em. But water running over a cliff? He couldn't care less. Besides, he thinks he's got a headache and maybe intestinal problems coming. So he says, "Go. OK? Just go." He's lying there on his back with his arm across his face.

I felt his cheek. No fever. "Let me see your eyes," I said. I was worried about hepatitis. He showed me. They weren't yellow.

"Let me feel your liver," I said. He lets me. I push in on it. Not swollen. So it wasn't malaria.

So I said, "If you get diarrhea, save a sample of it, OK? We'll see if you've got a bug or worms or something." He nodded without taking his arm off his face.

I've never seen Kit sick before. If he gets the sniffles, it's all over in about fifteen minutes. It's pretty much inevitable that people get sick in the rain forest. City people get malaria and dysentery. Loggers and miners get malaria and hepatitis. Indians get hepatitis and tuberculosis, and if they catch a cold, it lasts three months. Children get worms. Everybody gets dysentery. Nobody escapes unscathed. It's just a matter of who gets cured.

So I figured I'd take Soong Tan and go see this beautiful waterfall and come right back. Ronsh said it would take about half an hour to get there in his motorized canoe, and twenty minutes to get back downstream. I checked with the owner of the hotel. He said Ronsh was cool. No problem. I could trust him.

And I could. He was a real nice guy. He had this twenty-five-foot aluminum boat with a Yamaha engine. He brought his little wife and five kids and some cousins and two dogs. And a machete because, as he said, "Who knows?"

And off we go. First down this little stream to the Tapajós. Then up the Tapajós for ten minutes, then up this other little river. It was great! Just a few feet away was the real thing – the jungle, the primeval world, the planet as it used to be.

Ronsh and I had a good talk. As long as he talks slow, I can understand him. He understand my Spanish-Portuguese mixture pretty well, and when he doesn't understand, Soong Tan usually knows the right word in Portuguese. Anyway, he tells me all about being an Indian, which isn't as easy as you'd think. When I told him I'm a nurse, he tells me I should go to his village. Everybody's always sick. No doctors are willing to go there. No medicine.

Well don't you know it doesn't take half an hour to get to the beautiful waterfall. It takes twice that, mostly because his motor dies. But he gets it running, and off we go again. No problem.

The waterfall was beautiful. Nice clean water pouring from about twenty feet up and thundering into this nice little pool like you'd see at Disneyland. Everybody except Ronsh and his wife went swimming.

And then we came back. No problem. We get to the hotel, and there's this note lying on my pillow. From Kit. It says, 'Gaia's pilot is too drunk to fly so I'm going to take her up myself so she can dump her porpoises. Shouldn't take long. Goose can tell you more. See you later. Love, Kit."

Love? What nerve. And there I'd thought it was his liver.

So I go storming off to the cheap hotel. And what do you think? No Goose. They let me have a quick look in their room. Gaia's pack's there. His isn't. The owner of the place said she saw him buy a dugout canoe and start paddling down the stream toward the Tapajós. With his pack. So, like, that's the end of him. Care to guess why he suddenly took off? My guess: he was mad about something – same thing I was mad at.

So I go back to the hotel. I just can't believe the whole thing. I'm crying and growling and swearing vengeance on that bunny-hugging bitch. I couldn't decide whether to just leave the both of them right there in the jungle and somehow head for home with Soong Tan, or whether just to kill her and haul him back home and make him suffer until he's down on his knees.

But then they didn't come back. Four hours passed. It got dark. Where the hell were they? Twice I tromped over to the other hotel, expecting to catch them with their pants down. They aren't there.

There was nowhere else in town to go. Where could they be? Finally I thought of the airport. At least I'd know if they'd landed.

They hadn't.

Now when I say "airport," I hope you know I mean a dirt strip with grass down the middle. The control tower's a goddam shack with a screen door. There's two guys inside. One of them speaks a little English. When I first walk in, he looks at me like a stripper who just came on stage. He even looks at Soong Tan. Then I tell him I want to know about a man and a woman with a couple of big boxes who took off in a small plane. Suddenly his face gets this washed-out look. He asks me who I am. I tell him. He asks me who was on the plane. I give him Kit's full name and Gaia's first, which I can't even spell. Then I ask why he wants to know.

He says it's really nothing to worry about. This kind of thing happens, and often there's no problem. It's too soon to be really concerned about it. It seems the plane has disappeared.

I say, "Disappeared?"

He nods to the side. "Yes," he says. "We hear them on ze radio. In English. First ze girl. Zen ze man. I could not understand everysing, but they say 'Emairgency, emairgency. We are going down.' They say it many times. Then the radio stops. No more. *Morto*."

I didn't know what to say. All I could do is just stand there with my mouth open. I couldn't cry. I couldn't scream. I was speechless. I just held Soong Tan against me.

"Maybe zey are OK," the man said. "Planes fall a lot in Amazonia. Sometimes they are OK. Sometimes...", and he just wiggles his fingers.

"So...is there a search party?"

He leans in closer to hear me again.

"A search party," I say. "Is somebody looking for them?"

"Oh, yes. I understand. Look for. Yes. No. I am sorry. Zere are no ozzer planes. Only one. Another gringo has. But he has good pilot. He does not become lost."

"And my husband?"

"We do not know where zey go, what direction. He show me pilot license and keys for ze plane. I say, OK, clear for take-off. And ze go." His hand imitated a plane rising into the air.

Susan, I can't tell you how scared I am. He's out there in the jungle, dead or dying. I'm sure he wouldn't play around about something like that. I'm sure it's that bitch's fault.

I waited all day for Edgar. He never came back. Elizama got worried, too. We went back to the airport in the morning. They said they just got a message from Edgar's pilot. They ran out of gas at some missionary camp in the middle of nowhere. They'll have to stay until a boat can bring them some aviation fuel. By boat, of course, they mean canoe. A fucking canoe has to fill up a fucking barrel with aviation fuel and take it on out to wherever the fuck they are. Pardon my French, but I can't believe how fucking ridiculous this whole fucking thing has gotten. The guy at the airport says that would probably take two days, maybe three, to get out to the missionary place if they could find somebody stupid enough to go into the jungle with forty-four gallons of aviation fuel in a barrel.

Plus of course nobody's stupid enough to go charging off into the jungle in a canoe with a forty-four gallon incendiary device. Except me. And Ronsh, after I gave him two hundred bucks. I also promised him a gumball machine.

I know it's stupid, but what else am I supposed to do? I don't see any other way out. I can't sit and wait. I can't just go home and abandon him. So tomorrow morning Ronsh and I leave in his canoe. If you don't hear from me pretty soon, well, you know where I went. Sort of. That's all I can say. Pray for me, Susan, though by the time you get this letter it'll probably be too late.

Ysa

Chapter Nine

The Crash

All through his travails in the jungle, Kit kept a journal. He wrote it on the back of the pages of the flight book that was in the plane. He'd learned the importance of a journal when he was in Southeast Asia. When he went out on mission, he had to write things down or the days would blur into a meaningless mush. It was forbidden to write journals or letters or anything, but he wrote in a code that only he could understand, an uninterpretable mixture of Spanish, Pig Latin and words in English written backwards. That was so the enemy couldn't read it if he got captured. In Brazil, he just wrote plain English. He wanted someone to be able to understand it and to know what had happened – in case he didn't live to tell it. Mainly he wanted Ysa to know. He knew she would suspect the wrong thing. So he wrote it all down.

August 29

I hate to admit I've made several sequential mistakes. I equally hate to admit I am alive by luck alone. And I hate to acknowledge that I may not live much longer. I have inserted myself into a situation that is not completely hopeless but still far from sure. In short, these words may be among my last.

First mistake: taking off in a plane with no map.

Second mistake: believing a plane's instruments.

Third mistake: taking a risk without reason

Fourth mistake: Letting myself get sweet-talked by a woman.

A nit-wit, I might add. A certifiable nut-case.

Nut-case defined: Anyone who would take a thousand tiny porpoises into Amazonia in hopes of saving the rain forest. What in the world was she thinking? These are illiterate lumberjacks who risk malaria, cobras, Indian attack and God knows what else in their desire to make quick money by cutting down trees. Are baking soda porpoises going to change their minds? I don't think so.

Nor did I think so when she showed up at the hotel and reported her pilot so drunk he couldn't stand up. Of course she's crying. If there's one thing I can't resist – or at least couldn't until now – it's a woman crying. So I give her a little hug and a pat on the back, and she hugs me and rubs my back, and I get all excited like some kind of a junior high-schooler, when her hand happens to brush two inches below my belt. What kind of a magic button she found there, I don't know. I never knew it was there.

All of a sudden I'm drying her tears with my shirt sleeve and telling her that maybe I can fly the plane.

Big mistake. It turned out I could indeed fly the plane. It was a single-engine made-in-Brazil version of the Piper Cub we used to fly on observation missions in Cambodia. A piece of cake. A kindergartener could fly one.

Except a kindergartener wouldn't take off without a map, and if he had a lick of sense, he would have known that "Made in Brazil" translates as, "Caution: Instruments-Don't-Work."

The altimeter worked. The wind speed indicator worked. The oil pressure gauge worked. The compass, however, was erratic, and the gas gauge was stuck on full. It read full when we took off, it read full when we dumped our porpoises, and it read full as the motor began to cough.

It was a mistake for me to assume that I could successfully follow a river for a certain distance, then follow the compass to the drop site, and then reverse my course. It was after the drop that I recognized the problems with the fuel gauge. Half an hour later I realized the compass was jamming. I navigated by the sun and memory as best I could, but there were no recognizable landmarks below. Just forest.

I used the radio to contact the airport, but if their reception was as bad as my reception, they could barely understand me. On top of that, of course, my Portuguese was less than intelligible. I shouted in English and Spanish and what I figured was probably Portuguese, but it didn't matter what I said. I didn't know where we were, and neither did they. There was nothing we could tell each other. After a while I gave up. I had other things to think about.

I never thought I'd say I was lucky to have made an emergency landing in Cambodia. At the time, I thought it was the end of me. But my pilot, a Vietnamese who'd been flying since

French biplanes first flew in Indo-China, knew what to do. He didn't make it look easy. I never saw a man sweat so intensely. He'd never made a landing like the one he had to make, but he knew the theory of it. He knew how to land a plane in a tree.

I think I would have been less nervous if I hadn't had a weeping Buddhist in the co-pilot's seat. I don't mean in Cambodia but now. I mean Gaia. Buddhism failed her as soon as she came within nodding distance of death. Typical of the completely irrational person, she responded to the threat by screaming, "No! No! No!" repeatedly, as if her denial might make the threat disappear. It didn't. It just added a headache to my problems.

Then she thought she could find support – physical support, the kind that might keep her from crashing into the ground – by climbing on top of me. I've heard that an animal faced with imminent death will go to whatever extreme's necessary to mate, to make a last attempt to propagate the species. They will also head for high ground. Gaia was attempting to do both.

We actually had a lot of time on our hands. By the time I figured out we were lost, I figured we were probably, or at the very least, possibly low on fuel. It was a very tough decision, whether to keep searching for the airport or a landing strip, or to select a suitable tree and circle it until the fuel ran out.

So, for about fifteen minutes, Gaia knew she was going to die. She did not believe I was going to land the plane in a tree. Perhaps I was too honest with her. I, too, doubted I could land the plane in a tree.

As I saw her mind disintegrating under the stress, I suggested she try meditating, which she had told me she does on a regular basis. But she just kept weeping and denying the situation.

Suddenly she turned to me and wrapped her arms around my neck and began eating at my face and neck and ears. She kissed my cheek and sucked on my earlobe and viciously licked my neck and forced my head around so she could attack my lips. I must confess that I found it exciting. After all, I, too, recognized the possibility of death. As if landing a plane into a tree isn't hard enough, we'd still be in the middle of a jungle that stretched as far as we could see. I saw little hope of rescue and less hope of walking out. If we couldn't find the right direction by plane, we'd certainly never find it on foot.

So the distraction of a young and not entirely unattractive girl throwing herself at me was an odd and yet welcome relief. All I had to do, until we ran out of fuel, was keep circling. When I found myself with a breast pressed to my face, well – God and Ysa forgive me – it was as welcome to me as a man as it no doubt once was to me as a babe. I needed it. I wanted it. I took it as I might take life itself.

Need I say it brought some comfort to my co-pilot as well? She had the top of her granny dress pulled down on one side so I might take her into my mouth. As I did, she maneuvered to place a knee between my legs and bring her whole chest to my face. She caressed the top of my head, kissed it wildly as I suckled, first on one sweet breast, then, as it came from within the translucent mustiness of her dress, the other. Both were small, rounded, succulent and, under the circumstances, very sensitive and responsive. Her nipples swelled and pointed, and her weeping deepened into a quivering moan. We both needed that affection, that gesture of giving life and support.

The sensation was enhanced by the slow floating of the plane as we continued in our lazy circle. I had never done such a thing in a plane, let alone while in the pilot's seat, and I wouldn't recommend it as standard FAA practice, but one thing's for sure: it's quite different from doing it in, say, an earth-based bed or even on a raft in a gentle sea. It's a different kind of floating, a lofty weightlessness intensified by the nearness of death.

So I was loving Gaia as much as I've ever loved any woman – though I use the word "love" only in a certain sense here. It was a love of passion, or maybe the phrase is passionate love, and nothing more. It's a cheap and easy love, totally engrossing, undeniably pleasurable, but inevitably short-lived. It wasn't like loving Ysa, which is passion combined with that love of mind and soul, the love we call true love.

To be brutally honest, I was not thinking such philosophical thoughts. I was loving Gaia, or Gaia's body, with absolute dedication. The plane could have crashed during those moments. I would not have seen it coming. I would not have cared. I was enthralled. Totally enthralled. Her breasts were in my face, my hands were squeezing the thin flesh of her buttocks, stroking each tender bun, kneading them, exploring their curves, substance and texture as if I might never again touch a woman. And she joined me in my passionate reverie. She cannot be blamed for what happened between us. She, too, was foundering in the lust for life. She could not control herself. I don't know if her state could be described as orgasmic, but she groaned and shook, weakening and stiffening as my hands and fingers probed her in a frantic search for something lost. Her hands, desperate for skin, burrowed through my shirt like an animal seeking shelter. They slid down my hips and into my pants, digging deeper and deeper. I wanted her to have me. I wanted those hands to find what they wanted so much...but the plane's single engine began to sputter and cough, and even before it stopped, the plane sank noticeably. My hard desire died as quickly as the engine. I heaved Gaia off me and again became a pilot – a pilot and a man who, even if not officially married and endowed with offspring, nonetheless a man with familial obligations and a woman who loved him. I speak of Ysa, my one, my only...my reason to live.

The plane had circled far from the target *castanheira* tree, the tree of the famous Brazil nuts. I spotted it a good five hundred meters to the south. Its phenomenally broad canopy spread wide and high above the other trees. The expanse of its dense, yellow-flowered dome stretched a good hundred feet across.

The theory of what I had to do went like this. Without power, the plane could circle as it descended. I would circle the tree from above, as tightly as possible. As the plane wound below the highest part of the canopy, I would pull back on the wheel, raising the nose and lifting the plane with the last of its inertia. At the same moment, I would hit hard rudder to the side, rotating the axis of the plane about ninety degrees to face the tree. The plane would briefly rise and tilt into the tree, then suddenly stall, hesitate, and nose down to fall straight to earth ...unless, of course, there were a tree in the way.

By some combination of skill and miracle, the plane did just as I hoped. It stalled just a few feet above the peak of the tree, nosed over, and inserted itself into the foliage. There it stopped just as gently as could be, hung up in the dense tangle of branches and vine.

I don' t think the plane would be worth much on the used plane market, but we were alive. Gaia was barely still a part of our world. She just babbled through her tears and touched her trembling fingers to her teeth. We were facing almost straight down, but we couldn't even see the ground. That's how high up we were and how much vegetation grew between us and our home planet. It brought back a distant memory of a carnival ride I once took with a couple of buddies. It swung us around and around in a pod, like a pendulum gone mad. And then something went wrong, and suddenly we were far above the earth, stuck but facing down. It took them four hours to fix the machine and get us down. That may have been the last time I was truly terrified. Life's been easy since then.

I guess Gaia had never had such adolescent training in terror. This was her first time poised hundreds of feet above death. All I could do was hold her until she stopped shaking. We didn't get passionate this time. We just clung to each other as if the other might somehow not succumb to gravity.

Chapter Ten

Big Problem

Ysa did not know the details of the crash. All she knew, really, was what the air traffic controller had told her, which was basically nothing, and what Elizama had predicted, which was too weird to believe. But she did believe he might still be alive. Her only hope of searching for him, however, was to first go get Edgar, who was also in a plane that had run out of gas, except that he had enough sense to land on a regular runway, not a tree.

So Ysa hired Ronsh to take her and a barrel of aviation fuel up to the camp where Edgar was stuck. Soong Tan was supposed to stay with Elizama, but that morning, just before dawn, when Ysa showed up at Elizama's room, Ysa found her drunk as a skunk. She was weeping and moaning about losing her husband – she assumed he'd died in the crash she'd dreamed about – and, oh my God, oh my God, what was she going to do now. All she had in life was eleven deluxe recreational snack dispensers. So she stayed up all night drinking cachaça with lime juice.

No way was Ysa going to leave Soong Tan with a drunk, so, with all due reluctance, she took the little girl to Ronsh's canoe and off they went. Ysa wasn't happy about it, but what could she do? She was especially pissed off that she had to rescue that jerk Edgar before she could rescue her own man.

Ronsh didn't bring his wife and kids and cousins and dogs this time. It was just him, Ysa, and Soong Tan. The canoe was pretty heavy, with the aviation fuel plus fuel for the canoe motor, plus food for two days, plus Ysa's and Soong Tan's packs, plus a cargo of staples, like kerosene, soap, flour, rice, salt, and cigarettes. When she asked him what it was all for, he said, "You'll see." She figured he just didn't want to try to explain it. Everything she said, and everything he said, took a long time because they had to figure out which words the other would understand. Ysa's Portuguese was pretty good, she told me, but it was always hard to get all the facts straight. She wasn't learning it so much as converting it from Spanish.

Once they got underway, they didn't talk much. Ronsh sat in the stern, clutching the steering arm of the motor and studying the river. They sped up the Tapajós, then up a tributary that looked as wide as the Mississippi, then up a tributary to that river. Ysa and Soong Tan sat in the bow, squinting into the wind, hunkering under the sun, getting their faces so wind-burned and sun-burned, they looked like a couple of cowboys who'd been left out all winter.

It was a pretty interesting trip for the first couple of hours, penetrating the Amazon, going deeper and deeper into it, farther and farther from the kind of life you're used to leading, farther and farther into a forest as wide as an ocean. Ysa kept writing in her journal. She said she couldn't believe how many trees they passed. Ronsh stayed close to the wall of brush that leaned out over the water. Deeper in, where the trees grew tall and dense, the ground was pretty free of vegetation. It was too dark for much to grow. Ysa kept looking for a jaguar or something, but it was just trees, trees, trees.

They spent the night at the little house of some crusty old guy. The house was up on log stilts. The walls were bamboo lashed to each other with twisted strands of something. The roof was grass thatch. It was just one room with a little porch, all about six feet above the level of the river. The yard was a swamp. Practically nothing in the house came from any kind of factory. Everything besides a few cooking utensils, a hammock, and the old man's clothes were rustic stuff he'd made right there. All the colors in the house were earth tones of brown, gray, green and black. The old man was half Indian, half black, half white and half something else. He looked several hundred years old. "Like walking leather," Ysa wrote. He had three teeth in his mouth, earlobes that hung halfway down to his shoulders, black skin, blue eyes, Indian hair, two fingers missing, feet and toes cracked like old shoes, hands as meaty as slabs of beef. He looked the kind of guy you'd cross the street to avoid, yet he was an angel of a man and mighty happy to have company. Ronsh was some kind of relative. The old man served them up boiled manioc, fried fish, fried bananas, rice made with coconut milk, juice from a fruit called açai. He and Ronsh slept in hammocks on the little porch so Ysa and Soong Tan could have the single room of the house.

I just can't imagine myself in a place like that. I can't imagine why Ysa wasn't scared out of her mind. I mean, these two guys could have done anything they wanted with her. They could have raped and murdered her, chopped her up with a machete and tossed her to the alligators. There was sure no dialing 911. But she wrote that she felt safer there than she did in her own home. These were real men, she said. Her honor and safety were in her hands. If Amazonia is a lawless jungle, she said, it's the honor of a few men who keep it civilized – more civilized than a place where nobody's going to help you unless you pay for it.

Or so she assumed. Because the next day, things got complicated. Real complicated.

She didn't know where she was, of course. Way out in the woods, that's all. Upstream. Waaaaay upstream. Then Ronsh turned left up a little creek so narrow and winding that he could hardly get it around bends without backing and filling and bumping into branches that hung low over the water. He had to back and fill. Ysa was getting very worried, but what could she do? Get out? Tell him to go back?

She smelled wood smoke before they arrived at an Indian village. A dozen or so Indians were waiting at a sandy spot on the side of the stream. These were real Indians. They weren't wearing boxer shorts like Ronsh. They were wearing loin cloths. They had bones stuck through their nostrils. The women were bare breasted. Breast didn't even seem like the right word. Teats was more like it. Everybody stared at Ysa and Soong Tan as they unfolded themselves from the canoe and for the first time in six hours stepped onto solid land. It was like stepping into cave-man times. And to the Indians, it was probably like the twentieth century arriving in a Yamaha-powered canoe. Soong Tan hung real close to Ysa. Kid Indians hung back, silent. Oddly enough, the Indian women were crying. That was when Ysa noticed there were no men, at least none visible.

The village was in a clearing cut into the forest. It had six huge bamboo and grass huts as big as barns. Smoke wafted up through the grass roofs. Ysa took a quick guess that at least twenty people lived in each hut. Six times twenty is a hundred and twenty. Yet there were only a dozen or so people visible. Where were the rest? Out hunting? Gathering nuts and berries?

Ysa got nervous when Ronsh ordered some of the women to unload the canoe. After everything was out, they removed the fuel barrel by just tipping the canoe over and letting the barrel fall into the water. Then they rolled it up onto the landing area.

"Ronsh," she asked. "Why are we here?"

"We visit for a little time."

"But...how little?"

Ronsh wags his head the way Brazilians do when they either don't know the answer or don't want to give it. He flutters his hand, palm down, fingers spread, a gesture that means more or less the same thing. "Maybe short time," he says. "We have a problem here. A big problem."

She had already told him she was a nurse, back when they had gone to see the beautiful waterfall. So he probably got his big idea not long after Ysa asked him to take her to Edgar at the gold mining camp.

He led her into the village. The smell overwhelmed her. She had never seen such a filthy place, not even in Burma. Pigs and chickens rooted around the open area among the huts. She'd seen that kind of thing before, and even as a nurse she didn't see it as especially unhealthy. But the place smelled of human excrement, too, and the powerful smell of a dead thing infected the air. It smelled just plain evil. The acrid smoke of a smoldering cook-fire put a wicked edge on the smell. Then she saw the dead pig and the ungodly cloud of flies around it. Then she noticed vultures standing around. Like the Indians, the motionless vultures seemed to be observing her, wondering what she was, where she'd come from, and what she'd come for.

Ronsh picked up a smoldering stick of firewood from a small fireplace outside one of the huts. He waved it in the air to heat it up a bit and release more smoke. Then he lifted aside the blanket that hung across the doorway of the hut. A fetid breath of human rot and dry sewage swelled out. Ronsh recoiled, grimaced, waved the smoky stick inside the door, gobbled a lungful of air and gestured for Ysa to follow him.

Ysa motioned for Soong Tan to wait outside. She already suspected what she'd find in the hut. This was where they'd keep the old ones dying of pneumonia or tuberculosis. Indians were especially susceptible to these "White Man diseases." Even the common cold, when it penetrated Amazonia far enough, hit Indian villages like a bowling ball. By the smell that issued from the door of the big, high-roofed hut, Ysa expected to find someone in there pretty close to death.

The only light was what little leaked in through the cracks in the bamboo wall. Before Ysa saw the people, she heard the flies. They buzzed as if sharing a secret, as if not wanting outside flies to learn of the treasure they had discovered. Their trove was a population of people too weak to move, people well on their way to death. As her eyes adjusted to the light, Ysa saw the tangled forest of hammocks and then the mounds on the floor, people lying on mats, motionless and for all she knew, dead.

But no, they weren't dead. They were just dying. Ronsh led her to an orange and yellow hammock. An old woman lay inside, wrapped as if in a cocoon. Ronsh laid a hand upon the woman's shoulder and said to Ysa, "My mother."

The woman panted as if out of breath. He skin was paler than Ronsh's. With a nurse's instinct – and she knew it was a stupid thing to do – she lay her hand on the woman's forehead. Though under a blanket, the emaciated woman quivered as if freezing. The fever was mild, perhaps a hundred, at most a hundred and one. The woman's dark eyes opened a crack, then closed in silent agony.

Ysa shouted out, "Soong Tan!"

"What?" The girl's voice came outside, from near the door.

"Don't come in! Go open my backpack. Get my medical kit. Just leave it outside the door. Then go wait at the canoe."

"Will do."

That's what she liked most about Soong Tan. No questions. No backtalk. Will do.

Ysa took out her stethoscope, warmed it with her hand, then snaked it under the sick woman's blanket to place it against her chest. The left lung sounded normal, but the right worked with a wheezing rumble in the lower lobe.

"I need some light in here," she stated to Ronsh. In a moment, a match scratched. Yellow light flared up with a tiny, vicious roar, and then settled into a calm flame atop a candle. Ysa held it in front of the woman's face. With thumb and forefinger she peeled open the woman's eye. It showed a slight yellow of jaundice but not enough to indicate a serious case of hepatitis. She felt for the woman's liver. It wasn't firm enough to suggest hepatitis or malaria, but the woman flinched at the touch. She also flinched when Ysa pressed in on the area around the appendix.

Ysa didn't know how to say stool sample in Portuguese, but her suspicions led her to a dab of the stuff between her buttocks, a deposit inevitably left by dysentery. She scraped up a bit on the blade of her pocket knife. It looked tainted by blood and mucous.

"I'll need to look at this under a microscope," she said to Ronsh.

"No microscopes here," Ronsh answered, almost laughing.

He was wrong about that. Ysa had one, borrowed from the pathology lab where she worked. Her colleagues there had joked about her brining back specimens of strange intestinal beings. Outside, she set up her microscope on a wooden crate, touched a bit of the stool sample to a glass slide, adjusted the little mirror on the microscope so it shined sunlight up through the sample, and bent to have a look.

She saw an amoeba. Peeling through the tissue-thin pages of her Merck Manual, she found a description that matched the bug pretty closely. The symptoms matched, too.

"*Entameba histolytica*," she murmured. "Amoebiasis."

Ronsh, thinking she was speaking to him, leaned in and said, "Enta-what?"

"I think it is *entameba histolytic*a," she said, pronouncing the medical term with a Portuguese accent,"complicated with diffuse amebic hepatitis."

"Many have died of this," Ronsh added, quite needlessly.

Ysa nodded heavily. "Untreated, it kills," she said. "Where do you get your drinking water?"

"From the river," Ronsh said. "We always have."

"And what's upstream?"

"Several kilometers up, men mine for gold. Many bad men there. Very bad."

Ysa already suspected the source of the problems. "Do they come here?"

"They come. They pay our boys to pan for gold. They take our women to cook. They pay with gold, but what good is gold? The women come home sick. Sometimes they die. Others become sick. Gold does not cure them."

This pained Ysa. The disease was spreading not just from contaminated water but sexually. That complicated matters and explained the infections in the liver and lung. It could also get into the brain.

"We need to treat these people," she said to Ronsh. "If we don't, they'll die."

"Why do you tell me this?" he said. "Many have died already. You are a nurse. I brought you here to treat my people. Will you do it?"

"It's not that easy," Ysa said. "You need the right antibiotic. It's just a tablet, but if you have the wrong one, you can make it worse. I don't really know...I'm not a doctor...I can't prescribe pharmaceuticals."

Ronsh looked her straight in the eye. "I know this tablet. The gold miners have it. The disease comes from there. It is their gift to the Indians."

"The tablets?"

“The disease. They do not give medicine to Indians. They only give us disease.”

“Why didn’t you tell me this before we came? We could have bought medicine in Jacaréacanga...”

Ronsh shook his head. “No. They have no medicine for this there. Only in Belém.”

“Where do the miners get it?”

“A plane comes with food, cachaça, medicine. But no more.”

“No more what?”

“No more plane. It fell.”

“Fell?”

With his hand, Ronsh showed her how it had fallen, curving into a nosedive, hitting the ground and exploding. “Pilot died,” he said. “Now no plane comes. Maybe miners go away soon. They go or they die.” Just a hint of a smile cracked through his lips.

“Maybe we can go ask them for medicine.”

That made Ronsh laugh. “Very good idea,” he said, his laugh pierced with agony. “Brilliant! We will go ask the miners to die so that Indians can have their medicine. I’m sure they will like that idea very much!”

“Well...we could go there and ask.”

Ronsh’s eyes narrowed to glinting dark slits. “Yes,” he said. “That is a good idea. You go there and ask.”

She sensed the danger in that. She hadn’t meant for herself to go. “No,” she said. “It is a problem of the Indians. An Indian must go.”

“Indian go, Indian die. You must go.”

“No.”

Ysa counted four heartbeats before Ronsh replied. Still burning into her with his dark, narrow eyes, he simply said, "Yes."

Insisting, she knew, was not going to work, so she shifted into a tone of firm pleading. "Ronsh, you have no right to..."

"This is not a question of rights," he stated. He sounded like a completely different person from the one she had known just moments ago. "It is a question of survival. Not just of these people..." – his hand swept over the dozens of patients – "...but survival of our tribe. Our language. Our memory. Everything. It will all die."

"Why should this be my problem?" Ysa asked. "This is an Indian problem."

"No. It is not an Indian problem. It is a White Man′s problem. White Men brought disease to us. First the Portuguese, centuries ago, and now the miners."

Ysa drew the conclusion for him: "I think the Indian's problem is the White Man." But as soon as she said it, she took the thought one step further. The solution to that problem would be very bloody. Had Ronsh not thought of it? Or did it scare him?

If he'd thought it, he backed off. He placed the problem squarely in Ysa's lap. He said it not as a request, not as an order, but as simple instructions. "Go to the camp," he said. "Get the medicine. Bring it back."

"And if I don't?"

"Then you stay here and die with the Indians."

"And if I go and don't come back?"

"Your little girl stays and dies with the Indian."

Under any other circumstances, she might have considered this a death threat, and to her, a death threat was grounds for murder.

Threatening the death of Soong Tan made it grounds for decapitation. Ysa loved that little girl more than she loved her own life. Ronsh didn't know what he was messing with.

But he was already as deep toward death as a man can get. His people were dying, and unless he paddled away and never came back, he would die, too. Ya knew he was not the kind of man who would abandon his people. He was the type who would do anything to save them. Unfortunately, "anything" in this case meant delivering Ysa and Soong Tan to death's door.

The very air Ysa was breathing made her so sick she could hardly stand up. Flies with death on their feet were landing on her neck, her hands, her ankles, any bit of exposed skin, and she was almost to the stage where she no longer cared. That's when it's time to leave the tropics, she wrote later – when you don't even bother to shake off the flies.

Worst of all, she felt very stupid – stupid and guilty. She'd wanted to take a vacation on the Amazon. She just had to bring Soong Tan. For her education. And look what she got.

She worsened the pain by remembering how she'd smelled trouble from the time they left Belém. Elizama had even warned her. But no. She wouldn't listen. And then she decides to trust a virtual stranger and go charging off into the jungle in search of a man perfectly capable of taking care of himself. As if she might save him. Now she was up a creek off a stream off a tributary off a river and was being asked to do the impossible so that she could get back to the business of merely accomplishing the difficult so that she could set off on a mission most unlikely to succeed, and even if it did, all she could hope to get out of it would be the decomposed remains of the only man who had ever really loved her, and maybe the bones of the other woman who loved him.

Oddly enough, it was an easy decision. There was only one way out. Without lifting her head from arms, she asked, in words as cold as a corpse, "Are you sure they have the medicine?"

"If they don't, they can get it."

"So?"

"So…tell me when you're ready."

He clearly didn't mean ready to go home. He meant ready for Hell. She saw no need to answer immediately. She just wanted to keep her face down against her arms, alone in the darkness behind her eyes. She didn't want him to see her crying. She did it carefully, trying not to make a sound or let her breathing change. Invading a camp of cut-throat gold miners in the middle of the jungle was not a job for her. It was a job for Kit, but Kit wasn't there.

Chapter Eleven

The Porpoise

Just as Ysa was wishing Kit were there to save her, Kit was in his plane up in the tree with Gaia and wishing Ysa was there to bring some sanity to the situation. He knew she performed well under pressure. She did not let fear get in her way. She did what she had to do and did it well. Gaia, however, was a different story.

August 30

Now I know what it's like to spend a night in a tree with an insaniac. I will always wonder what makes women so afraid to die. Why can't they realize that they'll never be free until they're ready to treat their lives like something disposable?

I'll admit it was a rather hairy experience. The plane hung a good three hundred feet in the air, gripped nose-down by branches. I myself considered it rather thrilling to know that at any moment, with any passing breeze, a crucial twig could snap, releasing us to the pull of gravity. I like sleeping that way – light but not too light.

Granted, it wasn't the most comfortable of beds. Gaia and I

were basically up against the cockpit windshield. It took us a while to find comfortable positions wrapped around the (steering wheels --) and seats. We had to move very carefully to avoid shaking the plane and loosening it from the tree's tenuous grip. Gaia attained what might be called an altered state of consciousness. It might also be called a nervous breakdown. She just kept whimpering. It got to me. I kept my arm around her all night, offering what comfort I could.

But we did not – I repeat: not – get into the death-fearing passion that almost got us killed before the crash. I felt Gaia's fingers on my neck and on my belly, just below the bottom of my shirt, but I don't think she was in her right mind. She just needed to touch someone. If I'd been a gorilla she would have held onto me the same way. And I think that if she'd been a gorilla, I would have let her hold me the same way, too.

Come morning we had to find a way down from the tree. I certainly didn't expect rescue. I had to practically break Gaia's arms to get her hands off me. Still insane with fear, she seemed to think she might save herself by holding on to me. But I had to go out alone to prowl around the branches and see how we might get down.

I felt like I was climbing around a giant stalk of broccoli. That's what it was like. I was so far up I couldn't see the ground, just the sea of trees that rose to within fifty feet of the crown of this one giant tree. I moved very slowly and carefully, hugging each branch more tightly than I ever hugged Ysa – a fact I vowed to change, and not by hugging the branches more lightly.

The branches were slippery with moss and crawling with

ants and other insects. The tree supported its own little forest of moss, fungus, vines, spider webs and insect life. It made maneuvering very precarious.

Vines grew very thick where the lower tier of forest reached the bottom of the crown of this tree. From there I knew we could climb down. Or at least one of us could.

It took me a good hour to climb back up to Gaia and the plane. But that was the easy part of our escape.

"Gaia," I said as calmly as possible, "we're going to have to climb down. It's that or die here."

She was crying again, but at least it was a real cry. She wasn't wrapped in her subconscious cocoon. She said, "No, I can't. I...I'm afraid of heights."

"Then you stay," I said, hoping that would scare her. "I'll be back in a couple of weeks to recover your remains."

"My remains?"

"Well...you know...whatever the snakes don't get."

"Snakes?"

"Snakes, rats, buzzards, whatever."

She looked down through the windshield, thought about it for a second and said, "No...I can't. I just can't." Tears flowed down her face as if somebody behind her eyes had left a faucet on.

So I hit her. Once. Hard. Just right. Boom. Knocked her out. I cut off the seat belts with my pocket knife and tied them into a sling. I tied her wrists and ankles together with wire from behind the instrument panel. Then I slung her over my shoulder like a big papoose.

I was extra careful climbing down. The last thing I wanted was to fall and be found dead with a young girl strapped to my back. It was tricky with all that weight back there, but she didn't weigh much over a hundred pounds. Sometimes it's nice to have a skinny woman, but such situations are rare.

I wish I'd taken the time to search the plane for some duct tape or something – something with which to tape her mouth shut. Because she regained consciousness shortly before I reached the vines I'd planned to climb down. That's when she started screaming. Like a maniac. A lunatic. A jungle animal. Maybe that's why jungle animals scream so loudly. It's the maniacs among them, scared shitless as they swing through the trees.

In my particular case, the screaming was point-blank in my ear. Her body, soaked with sweat, shook against my shoulders like a hundred and ten pounds of Jello. I had planned to slowly shinny down a nice thick vine, but after about ten minutes of being strapped to a lunch whistle gone berserk, I decided to hurry things up. A certain vine climbed from our tree over to a tree about thirty yards away. Maybe by the theory of grass looking greener elsewhere, that other tree looked easier to climb down. So I cut the vine, grabbed hold, and jumped. I guess we sounded a lot like some kind of female Tarzan as we swung down and across like a pendulum. It worked even better than I'd figured. The vine loosened its upper grip and lowered us almost to the ground. The quickest way to get Gaia to shut up was just to let go and fall the rest of the way. Brush broke our fall, and we landed on a dense mat of roots and moss.

We survived.

As soon as I got Gaia untied, she turned mad. She kicked and slapped at me and screamed holy hell. I just let her. I could see where she was coming from. Some people just can't handle fear. It scares them.

She had an astounding amount of energy to dedicate to her little attack, and plenty to say about the situation. Somehow she neglected to consider that the whole trip had been her idea in the first place.

She was pretty much pooped out by the time she stopped, but the reason she stopped was as much a surprise to me as it was to her. It was a gunshot from no more than fifty feet away. That shut her up good.

We looked over to see three men, each holding a rifle, though not in an especially aggressive way. The looked like three scruffy-types from out of a movie about outlaws in Nevada. One man held a little purple thing in his hand. I knew enough Portuguese to understand him. He said, "Is this yours?"

It was a little purple porpoise with a parachute. Gaia said nothing. She couldn't even breathe. All I could think to do was hold up my hands and say, "*É dela*" – It's hers.

Chapter Twelve

Green

After the porpoises came raining down, the loggers wondered what the hell was going on. Then they watched the plane in the distance as it went around and around. They figured out what was probably happening, so they jumped in their motorized canoes and headed for the general area. Then they saw the plane go down. And the next morning they heard Gaia swinging through the trees. After that, it wasn't hard to locate the source of the commotion.

And everything would have been plenty cool if Gaia hadn't chosen that moment to get brave. At the top of her lungs she started telling these guys off, ranting on about preserving the rain forest, saving the earth, voting Green, going solar, stopping the nukes, standing up to multinational corporations.

Kit tried to interrupt her. "Umm...Gaia..." he said tentatively.

But she just kept going. The whales. The furry little creatures of the earth. The sky above us. The clean waters that nurture us. All the little fishies in the deep blue sea.

Fortunately it was all in English, so the men didn't understand a word. They just gawked in amused bewilderment. Kit watched her with pretty much the same attitude, figuring that as soon as she tired herself out, he and the men could begin man-to-man discussions about how to get out of there. But her big words gave her courage, and all of a sudden she was charging the men, screeching as if to kill.

"Die, fascist pigs!" she screamed. "In the name of Mother Earth!"

But it wasn't much of a charge. The dense mat of roots, moss, and rotten branches grabbed at her feet and legs and held them down like lead weights. She'd sink one leg in halfway to her knee, then plunge the next in just as deep and struggle to pull the other leg out. The men just watched her come, enjoying the flash of white thigh they saw with each step. The last step, however, was a drop-kick to the groin of the man with the porpoise, bringing him to his knees.

The other men were still in what-the-hell-is-this mode when Kit started toward them. He knew what they'd do before they thought of it. Before he got there, one man kicked his black rubber boot against Gaia's face, toppling her over. The other man swung his rifle around and stopped Kit in his tracks. Kit knew when to quit, or at least when to pretend to quit. He put his hands out, palms facing the man in a gesture of surrender and peace.

The man looked at Kit, pointed at Gaia with his whole hand and jabbered something Kit couldn't understand. All he could do was shrug and give the international sign language for "she's crazy," a twirling of the finger beside the ear. He knew the word. "*Doida.*"

"*Doida*," they agreed. They seemed to sympathize with him. Maybe they could imagine being stuck in the rain forest with such a woman. At least they didn't shoot him dead or kick him in a tender spot. The situation didn't seem completely hopeless – not until the men tied his and Gaia's hands behind their backs, marched them at gun-point a couple of hours through the forest, rolled them into a canoe, and raced off toward the logging camp.

"Are they going to kill us?" Gaia whimpered at the top of her lungs. The word blew back over her head to Kit, who sat behind her. He was glad that the man in the stern did not speak English.

"They might kill us, and they might not," Kit said, wanting to neither scare her nor let her think of pulling any more commando stunts. "I think in the future maybe we should try diplomacy rather than direct frontal attack. Whaddya say?"

Gaia shook her head, letting her long, brown hair dance in the wind. It tickled Kit's face, which he didn't mind as much as he might have. Given the discomfort of sitting in the bottom of a canoe with his hands tied behind him, the hair was a nice relief, a nice touch of softness.

"Do you have any idea how many species they're driving to extinction?" she said.

Kit hesitated before confessing what he'd never told anyone. "Gaia," he said in a loud but passionate whisper. "Once I voted for Ralph Nader."

"You're kidding!" she screeched. "You're Green?"

"I am not kidding. I'm as concerned about the environment as you are. But...we've got to be rational about it. A porpoise bombardment isn't going to solve any problems. Besides, one more stupid move like that little attack of your and these guys are going to drive us to extinction."

"They wouldn't actually do it, would they?"

"They kill porpoises, don't they?"

That shut her up for a good long time.

Meanwhile, Ysa's problems were just as bad as Kit's, or even worse. Kit was held captive by a bunch of loggers. Ysa was held captive in an Indian village where everybody was dying. To make matters worse, she had Soong Tan with her. She couldn't think just about herself. She had a kid to worry about. And of course she was worried about Kit. Was he dead? Was he off fooling around with a skinny chick from England? Would she ever find him? Was she risking her own life and Soong Tan's to search for somebody who was already lunch to vultures?

That was her most horrifying image, she told me. Kit's beautiful body being torn apart by *urubus*, the vultures that glided in vast circles high in the sky and stood around garbage dumps and fish markets like a bunch of morticians waiting for the end of a funeral. She couldn't help but imagine them fighting over his organs, savoring his eyes, munching on his tongue, flying off with his bones. If the same thing happened to Gaia, well tough shit. She had it coming. No that she had enough meat on her bones to please a buzzard.

While Ysa was wondering what to do about getting amoebiasis medicine out of the mining camp, Soong Tan was already befriending her Indian peers. They were showing her how to use a bow and arrow. The bow was as tall as she was, and the arrow just as long. The Indian kids were shooting it with astonishing accuracy, launching arrows across the full width of the village and hitting a coconut that hung from a branch. Soong Tan was obviously a stranger to the bow and arrow, but by the intense look in her eye as she drew it back, Ysa knew she'd get the hang of it very quickly.

Ysa sat by the canoe down by the river, doodling in the sand with a stick while she thought. A thin cloud of gnats quivered around her head, frantic with the insane desires of small insects. She did not swing at them. They were as much as part of her situation as the rancid air she breathed but no longer smelled and the heat she no longer felt. The jungle was no longer a thing of discomfort or fear. It was merely backdrop to real problems, the kind that came from cities.

The big question was whether to even bother trying to get the medicine. The men in the mining camp certainly weren't going to just hand it over. Somehow she'd have to steal it. The odds against success were beyond calculation. She just had no idea. She'd tried robbing a bank once, and it had not gone well. She learned her lesson. Theft was something best left to thieves. Her profession was nursing and biomedical research.

Still, Ronsh wasn't going to let her go if she didn't cooperate. The longer she stayed in the village, the higher the odds that she and Soong Tan would contract amoebiasis. They had food and bottled water for a few days, but eventually they'd have to choose between starvation and contamination. It occurred to her to grab a canoe and make a run for it, but trying to out-race Indians on their own turf certainly would not work.

So she pretty much had to at least try. That left the question of what to do with Soong Tan. Should she take her along? Would she be safer among a bunch of prospectors or in the middle of an epidemic? At least the Indians were friendly. If something happened to

Ysa, Ronsh might eventually take Soong Tan back to Jacaréacanga. God only knew what the prospectors would do with a girl.

The deciding factor was the stench of the village. She could take it no longer. The quickest way out, long-term and short-, was to go take a stab at the mining camp. She'd just go see what she could do. If things worked out, well, she would get on with the business of looking for Edgar so she could get on with looking for Kit so she could get on with getting the hell out of that goddam jungle.

And if things didn't work out, well, she'd just do what Kit would do – think of something else.

Soong Tan was now learning to chop firewood. The little Indians found this even more entertaining than watching her shoot a bow and arrow. It was clear that if she ever went into the Indian business, she'd be better as a hunter than as a squaw.

Ysa called her over. Ronsh looked up from a squat-down conversation he was having with a couple of old men, apparently the only adult males in the village. Soong Tan dropped her ax and ran over.

"Sit down, kid," Ysa said, placing a hand on the girl's shoulder. "We've got a problem here."

Soong Tan took a seat on a log. Ysa knelt before her. "Soong Tan," she said, "we're in a real tough spot. I'm sure glad you're good at tough spots, because we're in another one."

"No problem," Soong Tan sang in Burmese half-tones. "What's up?"

It brought such joy to Ysa's heart to see the little girl already wielding English as well as any kid from the American heartland. What a superior child she was – a gift from her father, no doubt.

You could drop her in rural Virginia or a boat on the Amazon or any Indian village, and she'd get along with everybody. And she looked like such a doll with her circular green eyes pinched at the corners, her broad Dutch jaw, her slick, shiny Asian hair, her rounded face. Who could help but love her? In fact, that's what had gotten her into so much trouble in Burma. The last thing Ysa wanted was to have a nightmare like that start all over again in Brazil. She trusted the Indians far more than the men at the mining camp. People who loved gold enough to inhabit some jungle backwater camp were people who could not be trusted with anything.

"Soong Tan," she said, "I have to go get medicine for these people. They're real sick."

"Like, no kidding."

"I mean like, they're dying. They're all going to die if we don't do something."

Soong Tan said nothing. She suddenly understood the seriousness of the situation.

Looking straight into the girl's eyes, Ysa continued. "I have to go to a mining camp upriver from here. I don't know how long it's going to take. I want you to wait three days. If I'm not back, tell Ronsh to take you back to Jacaréacanga. Find Elizama and stick with her. If she's not there, then you just keep asking for the American consulate until they take you there. *Consulado Americano*. Can you remember that?"

"*Consulado Americano*. No sweat."

"Good. Meanwhile, I want you to sit down and write a letter to Susan. Write down everything that's happened, every detail you can remember. Tell her where I'm going and why. Tell her about Kit being missing. Write everything, even if you don't think it's important."

"But why?"

"I just want somebody, somewhere, sooner or later, to know what happened. If you get back to Jacaréacanga before I do, send the letter to Susan. You know her address."

"Got it. Anything else?."

"Yes. This is where it gets complicated. You don't want to catch the disease these people have. The way to catch it is to drink their water or water from the river, or to eat from anything they've touched, or get their spit on you or anything like that. No kissing the boys!"

"Yuckers!" She made a face of utter disgust.

"Yuckers to say the least. So look: I'm going to leave you some bottled water, some canned food, some crackers and other stuff. That is all you are to eat. Nothing else. If you eat any of their food or drink their water, you'll get sick and die. I'm not kidding. You'll really die."

"No problem."

"I mean it. You'll die. This is the real thing. So promise me."

When Soong Tan crossed her heart, Ysa exploded with tears. She pulled her little sister in close and sobbed over her shoulder. Soong Tan's little hand stroked Ysa's hair. "Don't worry, Ysa," she cooed with the confidence of a child who doesn't know better and an adult who knows all. "You'll get us through this. You always do."

"I don't know, Soong Tan. Maybe not this time."

"That's not what Kit would say."

"It's not what our father would say, either."

Ysa's father had been as gung-ho as Kit and every bit as capable of pulling off the impossible. He'd done everything he could to teach his only daughter to be the same way. And she tried. She didn't take guff from anybody, and whenever there was something to fear, she knew how to face it down. But fear is one thing; deep concern for your safety is another. And Ysa was deeply concerned for her safety, hers and Soong Tan's. And, for that matter, Kit's, too, but she was so worried about her own situation that she hardly thought about Kit. He – whatever was left of him – could wait. Again she picked vultures scuffling over his bones.

Ysa figured the best thing to do was pack some essentials in her day pack and take the canoe alone upstream to the mining camp.

Ronsh pulled the engine off the long aluminum canoe and mounted it on a dugout about half as long and twice as shaky. He looked sad and serious as he adjusted the motor and tightened the C-clamps on the gunwale.

"It will be a very difficult mission," he said. "I understand that. I hope you understand the importance."

Ysa wanted very much to hate him for tricking her and putting her in danger. But she understood. She knew that, under his circumstances, she would have done the same to him or anyone else.

"The prospectors," she asked in carefully assembled Portuguese. "Are they bad men?"

Ronsh leaned his head left and right. "Some good, some bad," he said. "They have one thing in common. They all love gold."

"Are there women in the camp?"

"It is possible. A cook. Someone to clean things. Putas. Sometimes one girl does all three jobs. For gold, of course. The pay is good but the life is short. Indians say, 'Gold is Death.'"

"And what will they think when they see me coming up the river in this canoe?"

Ronsh forced his face into a painful smile. "They will assume you are a puta from Belém. You may be very certain they will be very, very happy to see you. A puta with hair the color of gold...it exceeds their dreams."

She didn't like the sound of that scenario. It certainly did not meet her expectations when she set off for a vacation in Amazonia. Nor had she foreseen it as part of the gumball machine business. She did not want to go to that camp any more than a cat wants a tour through a dog kennel.

But Ysa was a big girl. She'd been around. She knew the power sex has over men. She'd used it before. She knew she could do it again. Not that she wanted to go. she didn't want to subject herself to the situation. Men, she knew, were the most dangerous creatures of the jungle. They could be tamed. Domesticated. But like any household pet, at their core, in their soul, they were animals. Properly cared for in the suburban environment, with a TV and cold beer at their disposal, a ballgame to keep their minds busy, they were capable of behaving themselves indefinitely. Left to their own devices a thousand miles from clean linen, however, they would quickly revert to their natural instincts. Stir in gold and a woman, and the results were as dangerous and unpredictable as a wildfire in a wind storm.

So she was scared. Plenty scared. But she did it for her man – one man whom she knew to be as strong and powerful as any animal, yet as secure and self-controlled as anyone who ever bore the title man. For such a man, she would die if she had to. She didn't want to, but for him, for Kit, she'd run the risk.

Ronsh got the motor running for her, showed her how to set the choke, how to accelerate without drowning the carburetor. She knew she looked a little silly as she set off. The engine roared in high-pitched whine, almost tossing her off the stern, throwing her off balance so bad she aimed the bow right into a bush that hung over the bank of the river. In a few seconds the current pulled her out. She didn't look back. She tested the throttle gingerly, got the feel of the steering system, and accelerated slowly. The canoe handled well once she got the hang of it. She accelerated more. The steering arm of the motor vibrated almost painfully, but the bow lifted a little, and the breeze of movement cooled the sweat from her skin. She was getting somewhere. It felt good.

And there went Ysa, all alone, in a canoe, deeper and deeper into the rain forest. The river, fifty yards wide, wound back and forth like a snake, bend after bend after bend. Fearful of getting far from shore, she got very good at steering. The trick was to throw the steering arm hard to the left or right at just the moment that would point the bow around the apex of the bend. If she did it right, the stern would swing around in a headlong sweep that barely cleared the bushes along the bank. The vegetation seemed to grab in at her. Tentacles of moss and vine groped down. When she got too close to the bank, they stroked her with lukewarm dew. She heard monkeys screeching in the trees. She saw a green and brown snake swimming, wiggling across the water like a sidewinder.

Over the course of four hours, the color of the water changed from dirt-brown to clay-brown to chocolate milk. A thick slick of oil coated the surface with surreal colors. The trail of brown froth behind the canoe looked as permanent as plastic. Clumps of trash clung to roots and branches that touched the river water. When she slowed to maneuver around a log, she saw that it was wearing a shirt. It was a man, dead, floating face-down. She throttled back to stay beside it in the current. It showed signs of attack by piranha or God knew what else. She felt compelled to do something about the body but could think of nothing. She certainly wasn't going to touch it. After a minute or two, she decided she had no choice but to keep going. She'd report it to the next government authority she saw. Black hair, yellow shorts, a gray T-shirt – that was all she could offer to identify the body. It could have been anyone.

And it could have been her. She could very well find herself floating face-down in the river, slowly becoming fish food, a body that would never be found or identified. Soong Tan would always wonder what had happened to her. The poor kid would be an orphan again.

Or did women float face-up? She vaguely recalled reading that fact somewhere. Pondering that morbid question, she wondered whether she was going to find out the hard way. But she didn't stop. She didn't turn around. She didn't go home and take up knitting. She kept going, probing the throat of death. Because she was in love. Real love. The kind that stops at nothing, not even when it should.

Chapter Thirteen

The Hunter

Susan received three letters from Soong Tan. The first somehow made its way from the Indian village back to the post office in Jacaréacanga, which, despite a lack of stamps, sent it on its way to Virginia.

Dear Aunt Susan,

Ysa told me to write to you to tell you what's going on. Believe me, it hasn't turned out to be the vacation we were expecting. I thought it was going to be dull! And Ysa thought she was going to be lying around on the beach in her bikini. I don't know what Kit expected, but last we heard, he was in a plane crash.

Not that I'm worried. Kit doesn't die. The plane might have crashed, but Kit didn't. He's good with a parachute. I'm pretty sure that's what happened. He parachuted into the jungle. Right now he's probably wrestling with an anaconda or something. But that's OK. He likes that kind of stuff.

Ysa just took off for some kind of gold mine to get medicine for some Indians who are dying of a disease. She went in a dugout canoe with a little motor on the back. I cried when I saw her go around the first bend, but then I laughed when she ran into a bush and came floating back. But she tried again, and off she went.

So I'm still here in the Indian village. It's a pretty cool place. I don't think it's as dangerous as she says. The kids play a whole different bunch of games here. One's like tag, except you tag a kid with a long stick, which would be easy except everybody has a long stick, and tagging a kid's stick doesn't count. It's kind of like a running sword fight.

They also play target practice with a bow and arrow. Boy are they good at it! You should see! They can shoot a coconut that's hanging on a long string and swinging back and forth from a branch. They're trying to teach me. I've kinda got the hang of it, but I'll never be an Indian, that's for sure. One kid shot a teenie-weenie little bird that was way up in a tree. I can hit the coconut sometimes, but not if it's swinging.

I think they want to take me hunting. (I'm never sure what they want. I don't speak Munducuru, and they don't English or even Portuguese. And forget Burmese. So we use sign language a lot, and somehow we know what each other is saying. I think they said they want to go hunting and shoot a monkey. I'll go, but I hope they just shoot an alligator or something. I don't want to see any dead monkeys.

Ysa didn't say anything about me not going hunting. But I'm not supposed to do everything else. Can't drink any water but what we brought. Can't eat Indian food. Can't let the boys kiss me. (Like she had to tell me that!) Can't go in the hut where everybody's dying.

But she didn't say don't go hunting.

Get this: I could be wrong, but I think these guys poison their arrows with venom from some kind of a frog. The kids showed me the frogs. They're bright green and kind of skinny and small, with big red eyes. The Indians keep them in a little pit. When I reached out to pick one up, the kids went nuts. They pulled my hand back, and their eyes were as big as saucers. They acted out what would happen if I touched one. First my finger would hurt. Then my hand would hurt. Then I'd stop breathing. Then I'd flop around on the ground. Then I'd die and all the Indians would cry over me.

Shouldn't somebody have told me about these frogs before I came here? I mean, suppose I just picked one up? What else have they forgotten to tell me?

None of the men are in the village, except for Ronsh and a couple dying in the dying hut. The rest are off hunting, I think. Or on the warpath. I couldn't really tell. The kids tried to explain by drawing on their faces with berries and yellow stuff that looks like it might be sap or something. (Ysa told me to tell you all these details. If you don't like it, you can skip over them. I don't care.) They painted my face, too. I look awesome – or at least I think I do. There's no mirrors here. The only thing I could see my reflection in was a gourd full of dirty water. For all I know, it was their drinking water. I don't know. If Ysa should ever ask, tell her I didn't drink it! I didn't even lean in very close. It was so gross!

Ronsh is the only one I can talk to. He knows Portuguese, which I kind of know. A little. He told me my mother is very brave. I told him she isn't my mother but I knew what he meant. And he's sure right. She's brave and Kit's brave. So I guess I have to be brave, too. It runs in the family.

But look where the family is! I'm in an Indian village. Ysa's headed for a gold mine. Nobody knows where Kit is. I don't know why, but when I start thinking about it, I don't feel very brave. I just feel...I don't know...like, scared. Like something's going to happen.

Yours truly,

Soong Tan

Chapter Fourteen

Love in Chains

Kit and Gaia got taken to the logging camp. The loggers weren't sure what to do with them because their big boss was away and wouldn't be back till the next day. So they did the logical thing. They chained Kit and Gaia to a couple of trees. Then they went off to cut trees. Kit still had his journal – he'd stuffed it down the back of his pants when they descended from the tree – so he kept writing. He still doubted he would survive, so he noted every detail, hoping that by some miracle Ysa would read his words and understand what had happened.

August 24

The situation is rather serious. I have a chain around my neck, and the chain goes around a tree. Same with Gaia. Her tree's about twenty feet from mine, but our chains are too short for us to touch. We squat here like a couple of dogs.

I worry about her sanity. She has not taken the situation well. Though she no doubt considers herself a liberated feminist, her reaction has been typical of the old-school, unliberated female. She has been crying constantly and blubbering "No, no, no," as if denial might rectify the situation. She does not respond when I call to her.

Just as I'd do with a growling dog or a crying baby or a wild bear, I keep talking to her as soothingly as I can. "Let's try to stay calm," I tell her. "The worse things get, the calmer you have to be." But she just keeps moaning, "No, no, no." I think I heard her talking to her mother. That's a bad sign.

For the record, I estimate that some twenty men work at this camp. The operation involves a single bulldozer that pulls the logs out of the forest, a simple, open-air sawmill, and a crude log dock at the river. Best as I can tell, the logs get sawed into slabs a few inches thick. The slabs get dragged to the dock, and pretty soon I expect a barge will come along and pick them up. From here I can see that they've cut a good hundred acres from the side of a hill that rises from the river. The bulldozer hauls down a new log every hour or so. I can hear the chain saws just over the hill. The logs are massive, some more than ten feet in diameter.

From the air, this clear-cut area must look like an open and festering wound. These loggers harvest only the main trunks of the trees. They leave behind a sea of amputated branches. They clutter the ground six or eight feet deep as far as the eye can see. God forbid they should catch on fire.

Most of the men sleep in tents, which are just sheets of plastic thrown over rope. There's just one real structure, a large shack of rough-cut wood. The whole place looks very temporary. It's my guess that this is an illegal operation. Government authorities either don't know about it or have been bought off. I have a feeling that come rainy season, the whole operation will pick up and disappear.

The illegality probably explains the chains that leash us to trees. As I understand it – and I probably don't – we're waiting for the Big Boss to show up. He'll know what to do with us. I hate to think what his options are. I suppose they are a) let us go, or b) kill us. I have no idea which way he'll go or what his reasons will be. I wish I knew something about him so I could better prepare to deal with him. Is he a rational man? Is he thoroughly evil or merely greedy? Is he paranoid or confident? I hate this lack of information. It makes it hard to plan and decide.

In the absence of information, and leashed to a tree, I have no choice but to simply wait. I wish Gaia would come to the same conclusion. If death is our lot, so be it. That's no reason to break down in tears and denial.

I can't imagine what must be going through Ysa's head. At best she's learned that our plane has crashed. If I know her, she isn't going to just pack up and go home. I have a terrible feeling that if she tries to take any action to find me, let alone save the situation, she's just going to end up in more trouble. Amazonia is not for people from other places. We should never have gotten involved in anything here. Now I know that. The only question is whether I'll live long enough to make use of that knowledge.

I wonder how much help Edgar has been. I have very shaky feelings about any man so obsessed with financial enterprise.

I also wonder what Goose is doing. How attached to Gaia is he? I perceived a certain distance between them. I wouldn't be surprised if he was getting tired of traveling with her. Attending to her psychological needs must be a full-time job.

By the time the sun set, Gaia was weeping softly. Her face was still buried in her arms, which were across her knees. As it became obvious that we were going to spend the night under our respective trees, I coaxed her out of her psychological shutdown.

"Gaia..." I said just as calmly and soothingly as I could, "Gaia...I think we're going to have to sleep out here."

She sniffled and lifted her face from her knees. Starlight reflected in the teary bubbles in her eyes. She was exhausted from crying all day. Her long brown hair lay across her shoulders like a cape, covering her chain.

I thought it would be good to touch her. She needed a human touch. I crawled to the end of my chain and reached out. Gaia looked at my finger tips for a long moment before creeping forward and reaching out. Our fingertips could barely touch. It was just the slightest tickle, but it was human and warm.

I lay down on my back so that my legs extended toward her. It was the only way to reach her. Without a word, she understood and assumed the same position, her legs toward me. We were thus able to stretch our legs along each other. Our feet came to each others' waists. It was very comforting for me, and I'm sure she felt even better. Still, we did not speak.

I held her foot and stroked her shin and calf. She did the same for me. It was as tender, soothing and, yes, as exciting as any caress I've ever had. I fingered her toes one by one, knowing each individually, exploring their curves and indentations, the line of their nails, the bend and bump of their tiny, fragile knuckles, the valleys between them. Their undersides were as tender and nubile as the most delectable parts of a young woman. My fingers played with them, squeezing them ever so gently, plucking at them, sensing them respond. Each toe pulled back from my gentlest touch but came back for another taste of the pleasure.

Gaia has beautiful feet, small and graceful. I hadn't noticed before, but now, even though I could barely see them in the moonless starlight, I knew them intimately through touch. The instep curved as sweetly as the underside of a derrière, and the heel bulged with the rounded swelling of a young breast. Following its curves with my finger created in me the same kind of indirect pleasures and desires that are generated by the stroking of a beautiful woman in her most beautiful, womanly places.

How I wanted to kiss those feet! To take each toe in my mouth and make love to it, to wrap my tongue around it and nibble at its sensitive flesh.

I did not tell Gaia what I was feeling as I fondled her tender foot, but as her hand kneaded and stroked my own, she communicated a similar feeling. My toes stood erect and quivering with hard desire. They craved her sweet touch. The sensation shot through me, spreading heat up my legs, through my groin, into my belly. If not for the chain around my neck, I would have gone to her. As much as I love my Ysa, I could not have resisted the call of Gaia's fingertips. They raced lines around the ball of my foot, across the broad valley to the heel, around the indentations of my ankle, up a few precious inches of my calf – as far as she could reach. But she did not need to reach further. She had reached to the center of my being, to the place where deep desires are born. They were born within me, and I was as satisfied to have them as I was frustrated to not be able to act on them.

I don't know if it was her foot that crept up over my thigh or mine that crept over hers, but quite beyond my control, we each ended up with a leg extended between the other's two legs. Her foot pressed to my groin, and mine pressed to hers. As I rotated my heel against her, she scrunched against it. At the same time, her little foot ground against my thighs and scrotum. It was a sensation most tantalizing. I was as swollen with urgency as I've ever been, but I could come no closer to her without hanging myself. Sweat poured from my body. Droplets trickled down the sides of my chest.

She was pretty moist herself. I thrust my foot against her, as far as it could reach, again and again, pumping in a rhythm that matched her own heavings. Again I heard her whimpering, but this time it was not the whimper of sadness or fear. It was the heat of deep satisfaction filling her and bubbling from her throat. Then, suddenly, with an implosive gasp of orgasm, she jerked her knees back to herself and rolled to her side. Her breathing shook as she shuddered unto herself. She whispered something that I couldn't hear. Gradually her breathing slowed and her body sank into sleep. My own unsatisfied desire soon withdrew, and then I, too, was asleep.

Chapter Fifteen

The Ooze of Imagined Romance

About that same time all that was going on, Ysa was motoring up to the gold mining operation. She said it looked like a World War I battlefield after a bad day. Apparently the gold was coming down a stream that fed into the river. The prospectors had dug up an unbelievable amount of dirt, gravel and clay, broadening the mouth of the stream to an area a hundred yards wide. The stream now trickled through a web of canals that wound among muddy island plateaus. The prospectors, scores of very muddy men, stood ankle-deep in mud or knee-deep in water as they shaved clay from these plateaus and washed it around in broad, concave pans.

But they stopped when the blonde woman in the canoe purred to the edge of their mud. They didn't drop their tools. They didn't move from where they stood, but they stopped and they watched.

Ysa described them as a typical mix of Brazilians – a few with light hair and blue eyes, a few as black as coal, most a shade of brown. Some had the hair of Germans, some the hair of Blacks, some the hair of Indians. All were thin and stringy with sinuous muscles, and all had mud plastered on their naked chests and legs. As

Ysa put it, "They looked like they'd all missed their annual bath and had resolved to go another year without."

As she stepped out of her canoe into the mud, they watched her with paralytic dumbfoundedness. No one came to help her as she slung her day-pack over one shoulder and set into the strenuous process of sinking one foot into the mud and then the other, followed by a heavy club-foot of clay.

She did not kid herself. She knew she was going to get dirty. Very dirty. Once she had recognized that, it was not hard to become at one with the mud. As she plodded across the delta of muck, her legs often sank in to he knees. She was glad she had worn shorts. So, apparently, were the miners. With intense interest, they watched every step. She could practically feel their shared assessment. She wondered whether she would get out of there alive. She wondered how she would extract adequate gratitude from Kit if she ever found him alive.

She aimed for the apparent nerve center of the operation, a cluster of grass and bamboo huts on a rise above the delta. They seemed to cower in a nook cut out of the towering forest. The forest itself seemed sick at its fringe. The outer-most trees, stripped of many branches, stood as stark as cactus. A few half-starved vines rose from the bushes and clung to the trees like desperate, half-dead snakes. The wall of trees deeper in the forest seemed to trap a pall of blue-gray smoke within the encampment. It smelled not just of burnt wood but of excrement, garbage and metallic chemical.

Hell. That's what she thought. Hell would be a lot like this. Here all hope had been abandoned. Miserable people, dirty, hungry, lonely, sick and enslaved, were stripped of any reason to live beyond the collection of a scarce mineral which, once found, would only make them more miserable. These poor prospectors had not died yet, but they were already serving their time in Hell. At best, death might bring them release.

So their eyes, as they watched her slog from the mud to a slippery stairway of packed clay, drooled with a desire that went far beyond that of the merely lecherous. They saw in Ysa – she could feel this – they saw in her the touch of human warmth, the glimmer of human love, the soft company of a woman. They saw a meal cooked with caring hands, the cure of a mother's hand to the forehead, the liberating cleanliness of spring water and scented soap. They saw the opposite of Hell, appearing like a miracle, suddenly walking among them, muddy to her thighs – Heaven incarnate.

Ysa was a nurse to her core. She could not turn a blind eye to human suffering. She could not just walk past these men without briefly looking into their eyes and nodding a minimal greeting. They did not nod back. They turned their eyes away as if ashamed to have looked on such beauty, as if afraid to have remembered a world far from hell.

A man awaited her at the top of the clay stairs. He was relatively clean, wearing a long-sleeved shirt that might once have been white. Unlike any of the other men, he wore boots, black rubber things that came almost to his knees. With his hands on his hips and a revolver in a holster, he had the look of authority. That authority came through in his first words to her: "Who are you?"

It was not an easy question to answer. Her name would mean nothing. The man really meant what are you; where do you come from; why are you here?

But with her limited vocabulary, she could not delve into complexities. She just answered his question. –"Ysa van der Meer" – and let him figure out what to do about it.

He just kept looking at her, up and down, his eyes making one trip in flat-out curiosity, then another trip for the sheer lust of it, and another perhaps for signs of a weapon.

"Why have you come here?" He made it sound like an accusation.

She certainly wasn't going to tell him the truth, that she wanted to steal his gamma globulin. But she hadn't thought up the right lie yet. The best she'd thought of was that she was a nurse and had come to conduct a routine check-up. But somehow that defied credibility. It would put her close to the medicine, but maybe too close. The man before her radiated suspicion. The last thing she wanted to do was hint at her real purpose. So she looked him in the eye and said a simple sentence she could readily formulate in Portuguese. It was not far from the truth. She said, "I am lost."

At that, her eyes met his. It was easy to read his mind. She knew exactly what he was thinking. It was a thought as old as the animal kingdom. Though her arrival must have seemed to him too good to be true, the temptation was too much to resist. It was a crucial moment. It guaranteed her entrance to the camp. Unfortunately, it would make leave-taking equally hard.

The man gestured her toward one of the huts. The exaggeratedly polite sweep of his arm brought to her mind the phrase Step into my parlor, said the spider to the fly, and he seemed to confirm that feeling when he said, "The name is Rodrigo," and he extended his hand.

It was not the kind of hand she wanted to shake. It wasn't muddy, but it had dirt ingrained into it. The fingernails looked as if rats had worked them over. Skin had scaled off. She didn't want to touch it – she didn't want to touch anything in the whole damned camp – but for Kit and Soong Tang, she placed her hand into his, gave a quick shake, and tried to pull it back. He held it for a second while some sick ooze of imagined romance dribbled from the center of his dark eyes.

The path to the hut was a series of slabs of wood that had been shaved off the outside of a tree. As she walked along it she kept thinking of little Soong Tan back in the Indian village, alone among strangers and far, far from home. She might never get back to the United States. She might find herself living among Indians for the rest of her life – and probably a very short life it would be. Ysa felt the tentacles of tragedy wrapping around her heart as she walked toward the grass hut at the gold mine, Rodrigo behind her. Soong Tan, having been plucked from the hell of Burma and placed in the heaven of Virginia, might very well live out her final days in another corner of hell.

Ysa knew she could not afford a mistake, but the very weight of that thought threatened to grip her with panic. She tried to keep her cool, but she was sweating large-caliber bullets. The man was right behind her, his boots clumping on the long, thin board, and twenty other men were watching from below, all thinking the same thing.

Again with Victorian politeness the man motioned her into a hut. The air inside was stale and hot and tinted yellow by the light coming in through the bamboo walls and grass roof. The furnishings consisted of a hammock, a table made of planks across four wooden crates, a small, dented refrigerator shut with a chain and padlock, a radio that looked of army issue, and a stool made of a split log on four stick legs. On the table was a small scale, the kind with two pans suspended from an arm that tips toward the heavier side. It was tipped toward the side that held a tiny volcano of gold dust.

"*Senta*," Rodrigo said, indicating the little stool. As soon as Ysa had perched upon it, knees together, he lay back in the hammock, perpendicular across it in the posture of one in an easy chair. He put his hands behind his head to hold it up so he could see her. Broad seas of sweat stained his shirt below the arms, and the yellowish outlines of older sweat ringed the wet area.

"You are lost," he stated slowly, as if each word were a piece of a puzzle that had to be nudged in to connect with the rest. "A blonde comes a hundred miles up the Rio Mundurucu all alone in a canoe ...and finds herself...*lost*." He shook his head as if to shake a missing piece of the puzzle into the right place.

"Yes," Ysa said unsurely. He was very suspicious. He wasn't going to buy anything she said, not cheap, anyway. She'd have to work for his belief. "I am...a geologist. I am here with my husband. And other men. All geologists. And some soldiers from the Polícia Militar." She was surprising herself with her imaginative fabrication. She hoped the mention of armed men would hint that he'd better not mess with her. The little refrigerator beckoned her with the promise of a cold drink. She would have paid ten dollars for an ice cube. She understood why the little refrigerator would have to have a chain and lock, but she wondered how any machine could keep things cold in such a hot place, and then she wondered where they got the electricity to run it. The wire went right out through a crack in the bamboo wall. No doubt they had a gasoline generator somewhere.

"Geologists!" The man said it with a wide, toothy smile. She couldn't tell if he was delighted or just laughing at her. Unlike most men Ysa had seen in Amazonia, he had all his teeth and they weren't crooked. "Geologists from...where?"

He had detected her accent. Knowing that the best lie is the one based on truth, she said, "From the Estados Unidos."

"Ah, very good! *Geologistas americanos*! And you are studying the geology of this region?"

"Yes, we are. And I became separated."

"Ah! Separated. Yes, that can be dangerous. And you realize, of course, that you are deep in an Indian reservation." His eyebrows rose way up.

"Oh! No...I...um...I...I'm just a *geologista*. No map. I only look for..." – she didn't know the word for rocks. She made the mistake of letting her eyes wander in search of one. They came upon the little volcano of gold dust. Once they saw it, they could not detach themselves. It was a very captivating sight, a salt-and-pepper mixture of black and gold. "I only look for *minerales*." It was Spanish, but she knew he'd understand.

"*Minerais*," he said, nodding with agreement and subtle correction. "Gold?"

"Oh, no! No, not gold. No. We are interested in other metals. Umm, how do you say...*ferro*." Iron.

"Ah, yes, *ferro*. A very good mineral." He smiled inwardly, his eyes shifting low and to the side. He brought both hands to a pensive position at just below his mouth, one finger resting against his lips.

"How curious that you have come onto an Indian reservation in search of *minerais*." His eyes came back up to her. "There can be no mining here. Do you and your *geologistas americanos* know this?"

She was playing chess with a chessmaster, she knew now, and he had boxed her bluff into a corner. Suddenly claustrophobic, she panicked. She felt the need to say something immediately lest he see through her hesitation. She opened her stupid mouth and said, "But you are mining here, no?"

His eyes stabbed into her with cruel amusement. "Yes," he said. "We are mining here. And that is the problem."

Chapter Sixteen

Little Braves Go A'hunting

By this point, Ysa was in deep, deep trouble. So was Kit.

Soong Tan was in trouble but didn't recognize know it. She was playing with fate with the way other kids play with a puppy. She had charmed the Indian children, and they had charmed her. She was a really bright kid and just as curious as can be. So these Indian kids were showing her how they do all kinds of stuff, from shooting arrows, to making a fire without a match, to skinning a turtle, to making things out of gourds. She was eating it up like honey-dipped peanuts.

She was also eating up the food and drinking up the water Ysa had left her. Eventually she was going to have to eat and drink whatever the Indians offered her. She already recognized that.

As if hepatitis weren't dangerous enough, the kids wanted to take her hunting in the rain forest. They got their bows and arrows and dipped the arrowheads in toad poison. The bows were as tall as the kids. The arrows were five feet long and very thin. The arrowheads were monkey teeth, small but as sharp as pins. The arrow itself wouldn't kill anything bigger than a bird. It was the poison that killed. All the little hunters had to do was get the arrowhead into some flesh and then follow the animal until it dropped dead.

Soong Tan thought this was a whole lot better than the games kids played in Virginia. This was their way of life. They probably couldn't operate the controls of a television set, but they could take their bows and arrows into the woods and kill a peccary, a pig-like animal that weighed more than all of them put together.

And it was a peccary they were out to get. Soong Tan wrote it all down.

Dear Aunt Susan,

You won't believe what happened. You won't believe what I did. I'd better start at the beginning or you'll think I'm making it up.

First, you wouldn't recognize me if you saw me. I'm practically an Indian. It's soooo cool! My body's all painted up like a panther, and I've got a little loin cloth made out of an animal skin. Believe me, I'd never wear it in Virginia. Not even on the beach. The kids gave it to me. It used to belong to a little girl, but she died. They showed me where she was buried. Right next to her mother and her father. It was weird to see three graves right next to each other like that. I guess Ysa was right. People are dying here like crazy.

They gave me her bow and arrow, too, and necklace made of monkey teeth. They even gave me her name, too. They call me Mrypri . As far as I can tell from their sign language, it means "Cry a Little Bit." It's weird to be called that, but it makes me feel like a real Indian. I could practically live here forever.

But look what happened. Talk about weird. The kids wanted to take me hunting. I really didn't want to kill any animals, but I thought it would be cool to go hunting in a real jungle.

That night I slept in Ronsh's canoe, like Ysa told me to. The kids woke me up just at dawn. It was a weird dawn. The sky was funny, kind of rosy and kind of blue. Some of the clouds were high up and white, like long stripes, and there was this huge dark-blue thundercloud coming in. The way it all looked, it was kind of like a giant American flag stretched across the whole sky. I woke up worrying about Ysa. I wondered what she was doing at that moment, whether she was looking up at the sky and seeing a flag or something else.

The jungle was cool. Real cool. It sure isn't like the woods of Virginia. Not by a long shot. First of all, the trees are so tall you can't see the top of them. You just see trunks going up and up and up until they disappear in leaves. And the leaves are way up there, so it's like you're walking around in a cathedral or something. Except cathedrals don't have carpets several feel thick and big logs lying all over the place and swampy spots.

In places, the forest floor's a mat of roots so thick you can sink your whole leg into it. God only knows what kind of bugs and snakes are down there, so I don't recommend it – just in case a bunch of Indians decide to take you out hunting in the jungle.

And don't take boots. You'd think boots would be a main thing to take, but no. Bare feet's what you take. Because it's tricky walking. You don't just stroll down a path. You have to be climbing over stuff and walking along mossy logs and tromping through water. The Indians don't even wear sandals. Also, bare feet help you be quiet. Nobody can hear a bare foot setting down. But you might have to have feet like the Indians. Their feet are like real good at grabbing onto whatever they're walking on, like a log or a big fat root or something. I don't mean they're like monkey claws or anything, but it's like they can grip things with their toes. I can do it better than I used to, but not as good as them.

So we all had these great big bows and real long arrows and we go stalking off into the forest. There were monkeys all over the place. Up in the trees, I mean. They screech and howl and even throw stuff. They know a bunch of Indian kids with bows and arrows means trouble.

I can tell you this about Indians. When they're on the warpath, they move! Bare feet or not, once they get on a path, they practically run. And I don't think you could hear them if they were walking right by your face. It's a lucky thing I'm used to jogging with Ysa because otherwise I don't think I could keep up.

It was after about an hour of weaving through a bad stretch of roots and logs and stuff that we hit a trail. I think it was an animal trail. Peccaries, I guess. Somehow these kids knew right where this path was. So off we go, jogging along, swinging our bows, keeping our heads down below branches and vines. The forest was a lot more dense and low here. The smell was weird, like thousands of flowers in the kind of air you usually get after a thunderstorm. And it was dark like right before a thunderstorm. No more monkeys, either, so it was quiet – just the soft padding of bare feet across soft earth.

I kept thinking that we could have been cavemen running through the woods. I bet it was exactly the same ten million years ago, just a bunch of hunters with bows and arrows and no clothes sneaking through a jungle full of all kinds of dangers.

We were single file. I was about fifth, and there were a couple of kids behind me. All of a sudden the guys in front stopped short. Everybody looked ahead at where the lead kid was pointing. "What?" I asked (in Portuguese!).

"Cobra," he said. "Look."

Well I couldn't see anything. He was pointing at a tree, I think, about ten feet off the ground. I was wondering if there was such a thing as an invisible snake. The lead kid strung up an arrow. He didn't look worried at all, but he aimed very carefully. When he let the arrow go, it flew off right where he aimed, and all of a sudden there was this big, fat green snake with red spots on it wiggling in the air as it fell to earth, an arrow in its side. When it hit the ground it kept wiggling, fierce and hard, flopping all over the place. I was like real scared. It must have been ten feet long and as big around as a fire hose. I'm sure it could have killed me in about two seconds, and I never would have seen it up there in the tree.

So, like, if you ever think you might want to be an Indian, think twice. It isn't as easy as it looks. You've got to be alert and a good shot with a bow and arrow.

We jogged for a long, long time. A couple of times we stopped when we came to some fruit that I wouldn't even have noticed. But these Indian kids noticed everything. They climbed up a tree and dropped down some fruit which I've already forgotten the name of. It was kind of a cross between watermelon and squash, juicy and sweet but kind of pulpy. Basically you just chew the juice out of it and then spit it out. We ate some mangoes, too. They're the best, but you end up sucking stringy stuff from between your teeth all day long.

Finally we found what we were looking for: peccary poop. A nice little pile of it in the trail. The kids poked at it with a stick. I think they were figuring out how fresh it was. It was fresh enough. We were in the vicinity of peccaries. We walked a little farther and came to a regular little intersection where another trail crossed the one we were on.

Shooting a peccary isn't as easy as you'd think. You don't just stroll up to one and shoot it. You have to ambush it, and the best way to do it is to have a whole bunch of hunters strung out along a trail where peccaries walk. The hunters hide as far from the trail as they can, I guess so the peccaries can't smell you. For our particular ambush, since we didn't know which trail the peccary would come down, we had to have kids stationed in all four directions.

They used sign language and acted out the whole ambush so I'd know what to do. One kid got down on all four and trotted along like some kind of weird animal, snorting as he went. We all laughed so hard that we probably scared away every peccary within a hundred miles. Then another kid pretended to shoot him, but he didn't die. He just screamed and ran along the trail and turned onto the other trail, where another kid shot him again. And then he died.

OK: I got it. One kid would shoot the first arrow, and then everybody else would shoot theirs when the peccary came running by.

They stationed me up in a tree about ten feet above the trail. I could see about fifty feet up the trail. I'd have time to see the peccary and take aim and shoot. It was a real fat tree with a fork in it. I squatted in the fork. Talk about feeling like a caveman! It was like being a caveman and Tarzan combined. Which beats the heck out of being a fifth-grader at Beauville Elementary. I was up there in the tree wondering why we even bother going to school, why we don't all just live in the woods and hunt our food with bows and arrows instead of credit cards. But then I started hearing this noise coming down the path, a huffing and thumping that turned my skin to the worst case of goose flesh in the world. I never heard a peccary before, but somehow I knew it wasn't one, because if it was, kids wouldn't be out hunting them. But I stood up in the fork of the tree and drew my bow back and sighted down the trail. Whatever it was, it was going to take an arrow between the eyes. Unless I missed. I just hoped it wasn't something that could climb a tree.

Yours truly,

Soong Tan

Chapter Seventeen

Gumball Surprise

Soong Tan's peccary problem was nothing compared with the problem Kit had at just about that same time. His particular problem was a 9-millimeter semi-automatic stuck in his ear. There wasn't a whole lot he could do about it. His hands were tied behind his back and he had a chain around his neck. Gaia stood about ten feet in front of him, stripped to her panties, which Kit and several loggers were fascinated to discover were a camouflage print. She had a .38 pressed to her temple and a man's arm around her throat.

The man with the 9-millimeter was the Big Boss. He seemed to be enjoying himself. He was a roly-poly guy in need of a shave and wearing a T-shirt too short to hide his belly. He saw some kind of humor in having Kit helpless and Gaia all but nude and crying so hard she drooled. He used the edge of a machete to scrape sweat from Kit's forehead.

"Rather warm today, isn't it?" he suggested. The words were in English, a rather clear English, tinged with a bit of British accent inside the deep, stretched Brazilian-Portuguese vowels.

Kit didn't answer and tried not to look surprised at hearing his own language. That's his policy. Don't show your ignorance; don't answer stupid questions. The man's silence got the better of the man. He said, "I assume you do speak English, do you not?"

"I do."

"How very pleasant to meet a civilized person out here in the woods. I haven't had a chance to practice my English since high school."

"You were an exchange student?"

"Bully for you! My good man, you are most perceptive. You have guessed quite correctly. My name is Leon, and I studied at Exeter for a year. That was long ago, however. Now, pray, let me ask, what in heaven's name are you doing here?"

Kit thought it very odd to hear such words come from someone who held a pistol to his ear. He couldn't decide whether the man's experience with the "civilized" world meant more danger or a possible reprieve, a settling of the matter in a gentlemanly manner.

Despite the genteel words and invitation to confess his intentions, Kit watched not the Boss but Gaia, hoping to catch her eye. He wanted her to see him looking at her. He didn't want her crying like that. It wasn't helping at all. But he couldn't speak to her. That's what Big-Boss Leon wanted. He wanted to see Kit's concern for her. He presumed that Kit and Gaia were closer than they actually were. Kit himself wasn't sure how close he and Gaia had become, and the semi-British Bossman didn't know the complexities involved. He didn't need to. He had a 9-millimeter automatic in Kit's ear. He was trying to crack Kit by threatening Gaia. It was a standard device of torture. They did it in Southeast Asia, and apparently they did it in

Brazil, too, regardless of overseas education.

"Very pretty girl," the man said, pointing at her with a thrust of his chin. He kept the tip of the gun in Kit's ear. The hammer of the gun was pulled back. It wouldn't take much for the trigger to drop it. "A little thin for me. I like a girl with meat. But out here in the woods, we have to take what we can get. Don't we, old chap?"

Kit said nothing. He revealed no emotion. He kept his eyes on Gaia's face and considered his options. If Leon took the gun from his ear, he was pretty sure he could swing a foot out in a Tae Kwon Do move that would probably break the man's neck or at least knock him unconscious. Then it would take three to four seconds to finish him off, even with two hands tied behind his back.

But that wasn't possible if someone else held Gaia and if any of the ten other men who squatted around the scene could effectively interfere. So this was not the moment to attack. He'd wait until he got his hands free, until there were no more than three men near him, and no one had a gun pointed at anyone.

"Please," Leon said with sincere concern in his voice, "tell me who sent you here. I need to know. It's very important."

Kit wasn't going to answer until he knew what to say. The truth hadn't worked. When he told the man that the porpoises were a message to stop cutting trees, the man just laughed, and not just at his pathetic Portuguese. It was a big, round, deep-throated laugh, the guffaw of a fat guy who lives to eat and drink and tell jokes. Kit thought, then, that it would be nice to befriend this guy and go out drinking with him. They'd have a good time.

But the man was really serious about protecting his illegal logging operation. It no doubt involved local politics well beyond Kit's imagination. Suffice it say that the policia militar carried M-16s and that the arrested often never made it to jail. Kit assumed that the man had to know who was on to him.

"Please tell me," the man said. "Is it the polícia militar? Or the army itself? Or is it a federal agency? The Indian commission? The environmental ministry? The Banco do Brasil? Or perhaps it is your CIA? Or do you have a business interest in the wood? Maybe we are in the same business? Hmmm?"

The truth hadn't worked, and the wrong answer meant death. If he confessed to working for a government agency, they might well kill him on the spot. If he claimed to be a competitor, they'd probably make an example of him. At the same time, silence was virtually an admission that he represented something undesirable. He was betting that the man wouldn't kill either one of them until he had the information he wanted.

The man holding Gaia didn't show any interest in her, though he held her tight against him, pulling her back so hard her spine looked ready to snap. But the other men looked like maybe they wanted a turn. Her bulimic belly was pulled taut across her bulging pelvic bone, and her fatless breasts were pulled flat against her chest. Her face shined with tears and sweat.

"Tell him something," she wept. "Tell him to let us go."

Leon raised his eyes expectantly, looked at Kit and adjusted the gun in his ear.

"I can say nothing more," Kit stated coldly. "I am a pilot. She is an environmentalist. I only fly the plane. She cannot hurt you."

"No, she cannot hurt us," the man said with a smirk "Of that I am certain. But I am sorry to say, we will have to hurt her. You can stay here and think while she and I have a little conversation."

With that, he pulled the gun from Kit's ear, let the hammer down, and gestured for the other man to bring Gaia. Kit watched helplessly as they wrestled her across the muddy bulldozer tracks to the wooden building. Boss Leon went into the building with Gaia.

Kit wrote about it later:

> I knew what was going on in there. It wasn't pleasant. He was making it hurt as much as he could. He might well have been killing her in the process. Just for the joy of it. I can't express the agony in my heart – to be chained a hundred yards from the rape and murder of the woman I'd held for two nights in a row.
>
> The other men, the workers, just squatted around to watch the show. I gave them a good one. I could not help myself. Feigning indifference was of no use. The end was near. She would gang rape her and then kill her, and then they'd decide what to do with me.
>
> So I howled at the end of my chain like the dog they wanted me to be. I strained against it, bellowing: "Gaia! Gaia! Gaia! Gaia!" I hoped to hell she could hear me. I hoped that down there in that shack she knew she was not alone in the world. My spirit was with her. Though Leon was raping her, I was loving her, albeit from a distance. I prayed as best I could. I turned my eyes upward and asked God to do something. I questioned Him. I questioned His motives. Why was He letting this happen to her? I saw a dark thunderhead rising from behind the hill that had been stripped clean of timber. For a second I thought, 'Here comes God.' But I caught myself. It was not God, and God was not going to come solve my problem.
>
> And with that my prayer turned into the greatest and most uncon-

trollable anger I've ever felt. I turned and attacked the nearest man, a little guy the color of mud with black teeth in the kind of smile that just begs to get kicked down his throat. I leaped at him, but the chain stopped me short. Another two feet and I would have ripped his throat out with my teeth – and he knew it. He flinched but didn't back off. He just kept showing me those black teeth, watching me growl and strain. He had black snot, too, chunks of it in his nostrils. How I wanted to kill him. He was all that is evil in this world. He was the Big Boss in the shack and every evil man who ever wielded his dick with hatred.

Just for pleasure, just because he liked seeing a man driven to the wild helplessness of a chained animal, he shot me with a line of spit. Right across my face. Then he made the mistake of turning to see if his friends were laughing, too. That gave me the half-second I needed to swing my foot around and slam the side of my heel into his mouth.

He doesn't have black teeth anymore.

The other men stood. I knew they weren't going to let their buddy get kicked around like that. They'd been waiting for a good reason to beat the crap out of me. There were seven of them. In no way could I avoid what I had coming. But I was going to see how many I could take down first. I was already ahead by one. In fact, I'd already won the game. From there on, I was in it for the dignity.

They were careful. They didn't come right up to me. They knew I could strike at them only with my feet. So they inched in from all sides, each man ready to leap back if I came at him. I feinted to one side, then to the other, trying to keep their circle disorganized and unbalanced. I managed to get my foot around behind one man, knocking him down but not hurting him. He rolled away. The other men laughed. It was clear to me that we were in a battle of testosterone. To them, whoever won this one-sided battle was the better man. I already know who was the better man, but I was going to pound the lesson into them until they overpowered me, or a miracle came along.

The man I knocked down decided to do the manliest thing he could. He got a rock the size of a softball and, from a safe distance just beyond chain length, heaved it at me. Probably because they don't play baseball in this country, he threw like a girl, leading with his elbow. I had plenty of time to twist away so it caught me on the shoulder. It hurt like hell, but it didn't stop me.

At approximately this point in the affair I began to identify with a bull in a bullfight. The fight's fixed. The bull's outnumbered. The outcome's a sure thing. The only question is how bravely the bull will cling to its life and attack its aggressors. I doubt any bull ever begged for a job in the ring, but when they find themselves there, they fight. They seem neither accept the inevitable nor hope to survive.

Another man, self-appointed picador, came in swinging the Boss's machete, the one that had my sweat along its edge. He maneuvered it down below his waist like a baseball batter getting into position at the plate. I couldn't help but see it as the phallus the man wished he had. I backed up, giving myself more play on the chain. He came in closer. He looked very, very pleased to have me fearing him and cowering. His first swing was just as I expected – straight up, almost like a golf swing at my groin. I was ready for it. I hopped backward and kicked upward, connecting with his wrist. The machete flew from his hand. Before it landed, I felled him with a kick to the jaw and, as he hit the ground, a stomp to his solar plexus, knocking the wind out of him. Before the other men could react, I swooped over the machete, squatted low over it and picked it up behind me with my tied hands. A second later, I was in proper stance to kick the next motherfucker who came within my radius.

I sawed madly at the rope that held my wrists. It was an awkward way to hold the machete, and it wasn't especially sharp. The men's expression snapped to serious when they saw what I was doing. None dared come in close. One grabbed a rock and threw it at me, but again it glanced off me. I sawed and sawed as I prowled the perimeter of my turf, keeping them back, keeping them from thinking for the precious moments I needed to get my hands free.

Unfortunately, one of them did think. He scurried off to a lean-to and scampered back, lugging a chain saw in his right hand while his left hand yanked on the starter rope.

Maybe he was too excited. Maybe it was from trying to run and simultaneously start the motor. Maybe he was just stupid. At any rate, they had a hard time getting the damned thing started. I did what I could to hinder them. Still sawing with that dull machete, I kicked dirt at them and spit until they got smart and backed off. One guy got gutsy enough to throw rocks at me from a foot beyond my chain. I backed way up, hoping to draw him within the reach of my chain, but he knew better than to come closer.

Another of the ball-less bastards grabbed a length of lumber and started moving in. I moved to keep the tree between me and him. He was another deep thinker. He figured out that if he got me backing around in a given direction, the chain would reel me in. But he didn't seem to know that if I counterattacked, it would get longer faster than he could back-pedal. I tempted him with my chin. He swung hard, missed by so little I felt it whisk past my lips. Before he regained his balance, I was on him, in too close for him to swing again, head-butting him to the nose, then kicking him in the temple as he crumpled down, then pouncing onto his throat with one bare foot, pressing hard, cutting off the blood from his pitiful excuse for a brain...until I heard the chain saw roar to life.

A ghost of blue smoke rose from it as two men tinkered with the choke. I will always associate that smell of two-cycle gasoline with death. They got the saw running right and revved it up. The chain whirred around the blade as the motor growled like some maniacal animal. I must admit that at this point, I was no longer thinking of either Gaia or Ysa. I was thinking about getting ripped to pieces by a chain saw.

What angered me most was that they looked so pleased, so happy to see that they were going to win and I was going to die. The man with the saw slobbered with eagerness. His eyes gleamed with the quivering desire of a boy ordered by someone in authority to do something naughty.

At a bullfight, the real aficionados of the sport don't lust for the death of the bull. They lust for the elegance and the dignity of a good fight. The inevitable death of the bull is not the object. It is merely the driving force that infuses the fight with profound significance.

I think the men learned something when my hands broke free and swung around with an upraised machete. They cheered and clapped and hooted and howled – not for me but for the fight. It had turned real. I was no longer a hobbled bull on a chain. I could fight back. I could not win, but I could fight. They liked to see that. I decided that my dying act would be to leave them with plenty to think about.

The man with the saw had never attacked anyone this way before. It wasn't like attacking a tree. He held the saw before him, using two hands, more in the way of a lance than a sword, revving and revving. It was too heavy to swing, but he didn't really have to. He could simply move forward. What could stop him? Just to test the machete against the saw, I lashed out at the tip of the saw blade. With a quick spark, the chain just flicked it out of the way. If I'd hit it any harder, it would have ripped the machete from my hand. I tried swinging below the saw, aiming for his knees, but he parried with a maneuver of his wrists, punching the machete to one side and coming within an inch of removing my right hand. My brain flashed with the image of my hand lying on the ground without me, gripping a machete, jagged white bone extending from the wrist.

I tried feinting to the left, to the right, high and low, but the man was quick with his weapon. He was just fooling with me. Within a few minutes he was going to have the full hang of it and would know that if he simply moved in, I would have to back up, and I could back up only so far. Then he could have his way with me. Until his saw met enough flesh and drew enough blood, I was the mouse, he the cat. We all know how that fight ends up.

A single gunshot stopped things short. We all looked down into the center of the camp. The Big Boss stood with his pistol in one hand and Gaia within one strong arm. He held her like an oversized doll, her feet not quite touching the ground. Her hair hung over her face, but I could see her agony.

He hollered something and waved for the men to come. And with that, the fight was over – for the meantime, anyway. The men didn't even look back at me. The warrior with the saw shut it off, carried it beyond my reach, and just left it on the ground.

I was too exhausted to call to her. There was nothing I could do.

I just watched as the Boss dragged her stumbling across the camp. I feared he was calling in his boys for a gang rape, but then, as the men joined him at the saw mill, I realized that he something far worse in mind. Four of them lifted Gaia to a log that lay in a chute that ran down to the big, circular blade. The blade was rusty in the center but gleaming along the teeth. The men held her as two others ran ropes around her and the log. They were going to saw her in half, right up the middle.

The Bossman looked up at me. God what a smile he had on his blubbery, whiskery face. From a hundred yards away I could see the yellow of his teeth. He raised one hand in a thumbs-up gesture, then laughed and turned away.

Somebody started up a gasoline generator, and the big blade began to turn. As it accelerated to a terrifying hum, the Boss trudged on up to my tree. Before he came too close he used his 9-millimeter to suggest I drop the machete.

"Fala," he whispered just loud enough for me to hear. Speak. He was not longer trying to impress me with his English. He looked very mean and serious now. His little twenty-minute honeymoon with Gaia hadn't put him in a very good mood. "Fala, meu amigo."

I said nothing. I think he actually believed then that I knew nothing and had nothing to say, that Gaia and I really were crazy enough to just dump purple porpoises over his camp and then fly away, never to return. But our true intentions no longer mattered. He wanted to kill us. It didn't matter what I said.

The blade shrieked as it bit into the log, paralyzing the air with a noise horrendous beyond description. I saw Gaia screaming but could not hear her, nor could I hear the small plane that coasted above the camp. When a movement caught my eye, I looked up, expecting to see a buzzard already circling in. Instead I saw the impossible. It took me a full breath to interpret the sight and accept it as real. An absurd joy filled me. It was as if an old friend, or even my mother, were fluttering down from heaven under the wings of an angel. It was a ridiculous thought, but believe me, I have never been, nor will I ever again be, so deeply and instantly comforted to see a bubble gum machine floating in the sky, swaying gently beneath its parachute, its tutti-frutti-filled plastic globe glistening in the sun. Above it, headed away, flew a little airplane the color of a taxi cab.

Chapter Eighteen

Prey

It was Edgar Entwhistle, Gumball King of Amazonia. He hadn't known that Kit and Gaia were there in the logging camp. It just happened to be not too far from the Mission where Edgar had run out of fuel. Just by luck, somebody had shown up with a few gallons they'd stolen from somebody's boat. Edgar bought enough to get him back to Jacaréacanga, and then off he set with another gumball machine.

The arrival of an airborne gumball machine did not solve Kit's problem, not by a long shot, and Ysa's were just beginning. The gentleman she had met at the gold mining camp was not convinced that she was a geologist. It was not hard to prove. He led her outside, looked around for rock and handed it to her.

"What is it?" he asked.

To her, it just looked like a rock or, for all she knew, a stone. It could have been gold. It could have been granite. Ysa surprised herself as she said, "In English, we call it snitchpot. I don't know the word in Portuguese."

"Sneetchpot?" the man says. "In Portuguese, we call it hematite. I think in English is same word, no?"

"Hematite," she says, pronouncing the word in English. "Yes, sometimes we call it that, too."

He smiled, put an arm around her shoulders and guided her toward a hut that seemed to be sweating smoke. It smelled of pork and beans. "You are a *geologista*," he said, holding her close to his side, buddy-like, "and I am the president of CitiBank. Unhappily, I have been assigned to manage this little mining operation here in the jungle. It's a big change from New York! Yes! But when we are given a job to do, we must do it. Don't you agree?"

Ysa had a very strong urge to topple the president of CitiBank into the mud, him and his patronizing paternalism, his buddy-buddy arm over the shoulders. If he didn't like the geologist story, why didn't he just say so? Why didn't he just shoot her and be done with it?

"Yes," she said. "We must do what we must do."

"Very good. Very good. And we have a perfect job for a lost geologist."

They came around the side of the smoking hut. The area behind it was a rustic outdoor kitchen. A wood fire heated two steamy pots on a mud stove that had the dimensions of a large coffin. A tired-looking girl sat at a crude table, sorting through a pile of black turtle beans. She was a classic *cabocla*, a sultry, swarthy mixture of black, white and Indian. Her skin was the color of a serious tan, her hair a smooth oriental black, her face trim and small-featured. She didn't look up until the man said, "Elsi? I'd like you to meet..." – he looked at Ysa – "I'm sorry...I've already forgotten your name".

"Maria," Ysa said. She had no idea why she was lying.

"Maria," the man concluded, obviously not believing her. Ysa decided right there that she would never again try lying. She never had before, and now she remembered why. It was because no one ever believed her.

"Maria is our new assistant cook," he continued. "Please, give her some work to do."

With that, he walked away. Elsi showed no interest whatsoever. Head down, hidden behind a curtain of hair, she looked just as sad and miserable as could be. With minimal energy, she just kept picking through her beans, separating tiny stones and beans that looked a little rotten. Flies walked on the brown skin of her arms and legs. She wore only a sleeveless blouse and a short, raggedy yellow skirt. A green lizard stood frozen just a few inches from her bare foot.

Ysa didn't especially want the job of assistant cook. Especially not in a place like this. Nor did Elsi seem to want an assistant cook.

Ysa pulled a plastic bucket over to the table, turned it over, wiped the bottom with her hand, sat on it, started picking through the beans. Without trying, without caring in the least, she went through them twice as fast as Elsi. The poor girl moved with agonizing lethargy. Her absence of energy made the effort of selecting a bean and sliding it aside look like the moving of a boulder across a vast plain. Still without a word to Ysa, she lay her head down on one arm. The other arm continued to lackadaisically drag the beans away from the tiny stones. Her long, shiny black hair covered her face like a thin blanket.

"How much time you are here?" Ysa asked, trying to construct the sentence in correct Portuguese.

The girl seemed not to hear, and only after several seconds did she respond with a sleepy moan that seemed to say, "Hmm?" One eye glinted darkly from under its curtain of hair.

"How much time are you here? At the mine. Much time?"

"Don't know," the girl squeaked with weak despondency. "Much time."

The next time she reached for a bean, Elsi's fingers found Ysa's. She coaxed one hand over and looked at Ysa's fingernails. They still had most of the rainbow polish on them. Eli's finger caressed the colors. "So beautiful," she said. "So beautiful."

Then Ysa noticed Elsi's fingernails. The pale skin behind them had a yellowish tint. She reached to part the girl's hair from her face. She did not react except to shift her eyes to look back. The whites of those eyes were the color of pus, and Ysa's fingers felt the fever.

"Elsi," Ysa whispered, "you have hepatitis."

"Yeah...I know." She looked only a little sad to admit it. "I have many things."

"Do you understand what that means?"

Elsi's little smile forced her eyes closed. Without opening them, she said, "Yes. It means I don't have to work in the nightclub. Nobody will touch me." He smile oozed with satisfaction.

"Nightclub?" Ysa said incredulously. She knew the word from her days in Belém. Elizama was always talking about nightclubs. "You have a nightclub here?"

Elsi cackled weakly. "It's a small thing," she said. "Look for yourself." The faintest movement of her head indicated the grass hut behind her.

Ysa got up and looked in. It was no bigger than a two-car garage. The wall on the far side had a door to another, smaller room. In the dim light she could see one end of a tattered hammock draped across it. Somehow it looked sad. It looked like Elsi, soft and low-slung, exhausted and weak with disease.

"Elsi, do they know you have hepatitis?"

"Oh, yes," she cackled. "They know."

"And they give you no medicine?"

"Only for the men. They say if I want medicine, I can go away."

"Why don't you go?"

"How? Walk on the water? Fly like a bird? Take a taxi?" She laughed silently. It was just a shuddering of her shoulders. She was still draped across the table beside the beans. "Taxi!" she shouted quietly, almost giggling. A finger rose an inch from the table. "Taxi!"

Ysa always had a soft-spot for babies and lost kittens and wounded birds and such, and now she had a tremendous urge to put her arms around poor little Elsi and comfort her like a small child with the sniffles. She put one hand to Elsi's hot face.

"Where do they keep the medicine?" she asked.

"In Rodrigo's house."

Ysa envisioned the hut where the man had questioned her. She searched it in her mind, looking behind the hammock, under the table, back in a corner, under something, in the little refrigerator...yes, of course...in the refrigerator...the one with the chain and padlock.

She could see it in her mind, but she couldn't remember whether the padlock needed a combination or a key. It was old, she remembered that. It had a patina of rust across it and probably weighed a good five pounds or more. She recalled it as vaguely medieval, the kind of lock you could pick if you knew how. Which she didn't. She needed the key, and she was ready to do anything to get it.

Here's what she wrote later:

Susan:

Have you ever been in one of those positions where if you did just one little thing wrong, a lot of people were going to die? I guess it would be like piloting a passenger jet when it's out of fuel and on fire and half a wing has fallen off and the radio doesn't work and you're going to have to crash-land into shark infested waters during a hurricane.

It was like that, only worse. I'll spare you the details. Suffice it to say I had to swipe a key and then use it to swipe medicine from a refrigerator and then make my getaway in a canoe.

I'm not sure how it happened, but all of a sudden I was the camp cook and whore. They had used up Elsi, the girl who had this job before I came along. They had just milked her for all she had. Now that she was too sick to screw, they just cast her aside like an empty beer can. It was just a matter of time until her tattered remains gave up her ghost.

Meanwhile, they expected me to fill her shoes. Not that she actually had any shoes. I guess it would be more correct that they expected me to fill her hammock. The one in the "nightclub."

It was a cross between something from the Island of Gilligan and the Island of Dr. No. It was just a hut, maybe thirty feet by twenty feet, with walls of bamboo slats and a roof of palm fronds. Dirt floor. For furniture, it only had a long table with benches, all made of split logs. For drinks, it only had lukewarm sugarcane hootch. For food, it offered nothing. For entertainment, it offered me.

The guys started coming in at sunset. They picked up plates of rice and beans from the back of the hut and went off to sit under a tree and eat. Then they all had a smoke and sat around laughing. Then they moseyed on into the club.

Yours truly, professional serving wench, brought them doses of cachaça, two or three fingers of the stuff in a regular water glass. They'd down it all in two or three gulps, then wipe their lips with their forearms. It didn't take long for them to get pretty soused.

At first they were kind of timid around me. They couldn't figure it. What was a gringa doing in their little hellhole in the middle of the jungle? At least that's what it looked like they were thinking. But once they got a bellyful of booze, they loosened up.

A lot. Like I mean they decided I might like it if they kind of pinched me as I walked by. My big mistake was letting the first guy get away with a little patty-pat on the rump. I thought it would be hint enough if I just walked away from him. But around here, you have to do your hinting with a pistol.

I kept wondering how I was going to get the key from the Rodrigo. The hammock in the other room was in there waiting for me. I knew what these men had in mind. I could see it in their eyes, which in the faint glow of kerosene lamps were a bleary blend of yellow and red.

So I stayed outside, out in the kitchen area, as much as I could.

Elsi was out there, half dead, half alive, half asleep. Fucked to death. Those were the words I thought when I looked at her. She'd been fucked to death. She just hadn't died yet. But the day was not far off.

I decided I'd better level with her.

"Elsi," I said, pulling up a stool at the table behind the hut and laying my hand on her jet black hair. Her head was down on the table, cradled in her arms. Her face actually looked peaceful. It had a certain baby aspect to it. "Elsi, listen. I'm a nurse. I can cure you. But I need the medicine, the stuff in Rodrigo's refrigerator."

"Mmm," Elsi purred, a sleepy agreement that took no energy. She didn't even open her eyes.

"Where's the key, Elsi? Do you know?" Ysa was almost whispering directly into Elsi's ear.

"Rodrigo...in his pocket," Elsi moaned. "But he will kill you."

I'd pretty much assumed that. But I also pretty much assumed I should have died long ago. In a weird way, that's a comfortable feeling. Once you know you should already be dead, every moment after that is a gift. An extra. So I figured I'd go for the key. Somehow.

I hate to admit how quickly the basic plan came to my mind. I just had to get his pants off. Then it would be relatively easy to get my hand into his pocket. After that, I'd just play it by ear.

But I was still tempted by Plan B: to just get back in my canoe, get back to the Indian village, grab Soong Tan and head for home. I mean, after all, I was putting myself at risk basically for these Indians. And where were they now that I was at risk? I couldn't think of a real good reason to still go after the medicine...until Elsi, in her weak, babyish voice, squeaked, "Can you really cure me?"

It almost broke my heart. Poor kid. All alone, up in the jungle, abused, despised. I saw the dark bubble of a tear in her eye. I said, "With the medicine, yes, I can cure you." Actually there wasn't much I could do for her hepatitis, but antibiotics might help some of her other ailments, which no doubt included every venereal disease ever invented by man.

"And can you take me from here?" she purred.

"Yes."

She said nothing else. I think she just passed out, surrendered to sleep in the way of a child who leaves all problems to mommy.

Just what I needed: another kid.

Inside, the men were banging on their table and bawling for more cachaça. I took the jug back in. The room was so full of cigarette smoke I could hardly breathe. The smoke hung up high near the ceiling, heavy and blue. The men hooted like animals when they saw the jug. I poured a full glass for everybody. With each glass I hoped it would be enough to kill them or at least put them to sleep. These were the guys who had killed Elsi for the pleasure of their cocks. The only possible good thing about her hepatitis was that she'd probably given it to each of them. If there was an innocent man among them, he could find some comfort in his health.

When all the men raised their glasses in a toast I did not understand but instinctively suspected related to me, I thought they'd soon be asleep. The cachaça had to be a hundred proof. Six ounces of the stuff had to put anybody under, especially if they'd already drunk at least that much. And by God they all drank it as if it were water. The room was silent for the three seconds it took them to down it. Then eight or ten knocks on wood rang out as they slapped their glasses down, and then they all gasped for air.

I thought it would be a good moment to wait outside, but as I headed for the door, one of the guys grabbed me at the wrist. I pulled to get away, but he yanked me back like a fish on a hook. Before I could regain my balance, he twirled me into his lap. The other men rose up in cheer and pounded on the table with the kind of glee you'd expect from inebriated Vikings. Except these were Vikings in bare feet and ragged shorts, their bare torsos glistening with sweat, their skin dark by race, tan or dirt, their teeth blackened and broken, their bodies gaunt from hard work and bony from malnutrition and disease. Susan, you'd cross the street to keep from passing men like this. You haven't smelled man-stink till you've gotten a noseful of a man who hasn't bathed in a few weeks, who's been shoveling mud all day, who sleeps in the same clothes he works in, who's been drinking cachaça and smoking black tobacco. If they ever did an environmental impact statement on this guy, he'd be taken away as toxic waste. And there I was in his lap, and he was closing in for a kiss. The kiss of death. That's what I was thinking. If his lips touched mine, I was going to fall down dead from disgust alone.

He had one of his leathery brown paws up on my chest while the other snaked up the back of my shirt. I pushed at the one on my breast, but it was all muscle and very hungry for a taste of nipple. He enjoyed the movement of my hand, I could tell, and I felt his hunger swelling under my legs. His tongue was coming at me as wickedly as an eel when a strong hand clamped onto my arm and pulled me away.

The quickness of it brought barbarian guffaws from the crowd. I found myself plastered up against a younger man, not quite as dirty, not smelling quite so bad, maybe even smelling a bit of distant soap. His mop of curly dark hair hung over his forehead in a puckish, unkempt way. I could not resist – he held me so tight my feet left the ground – as he pulled me to an open space between the table and the back room, the one with the hammock.

"Dança," he whispered with a certain urgency.

Dance? With no music?

But he held me in a certain sensuous way, firmly, inescapably, but without hurting. I wasn't sure if he was holding me against him or him against me. His cheek, smooth as a boy's, lay against mine. He swayed gently, turning slowly, as if he heard music. Maybe I could hear it, too. I don't know, but I was dancing in quite the same rhythm. Somebody threw a glass of cachaça at us, but it missed, just spraying us with a quick, sour sprinkle before clunking against a wall and down to the floor. My partner didn't flinch, though I could feel his eyes glaring over my shoulder at the other men. The noise level dropped a few decibels.

Without a word, he eased me to the wall and then through the door into the other room. His foot flicked the bamboo door shut behind us. When he pulled my waist toward him, I slid my hands to the front of his shoulders. I wasn't ready for him, but I didn't have the words. All I said was, "Não...por favor."

He stroked my hair. I saw moisture in his eyes, not tears but a palpable tenderness. "You must leave here," he said, his eyes avoiding mine. "You must go. These men...what they do is below the decency of dogs."

He had not been long in the camp. I could tell. His hands, while not smooth, lacked the reptilian calluses of the others. The dirt of daily work had not ingrained itself into his skin. He was not yet an animal.

Nor, for that matter, was he a man. He was just a boy, maybe seventeen or eighteen, still in possession of a certain respect and tenderness. At the same, he was old enough to appreciate the softness of a woman in his arms. He wasn't letting me go.

"I need to see Rodrigo," I said. "Then I need my canoe and some gasoline."

He said nothing as his hands caressed my shoulders and back. He wanted me flush against to his body, I knew. I'm not sure if I wanted the same, but if I did, it might have been for much the same reason. Maybe I needed someone to hold me, and maybe I just needed help. Whatever the reason, I wrapped my arms around his torso and pressed my thighs against his. One of his needs became immediately apparent. It pressed against my abdomen with blunt insistence.

"Por favor," he whispered as his hand pulled the side of my head to his lips. They moved against my temple as softly as the paws of a kitten. They trembled with desire and desperation. "Por favor. I need you. I am very sorry. But I need you. I need a woman."

His hands descended to the small of my back and then, after hesitating, inched to my bottom. Why, under such circumstances, the touch felt good, I did not know. But somehow I was glad his fingers were kneading me, lifting me, exploring me, looking for something and, as far as I could tell, finding it. A heat rose within me. It shouldn't have, but it did. I guess I, too, needed human affection. In a zone of cutthroat immorality, a person needs nothing more than the touch of another person.

His lips pressed against my temple, and his tongue wet the thin curl that hung there. As his breath boiled against me, it penetrated as sharply as a hot knife but as lusciously as hot soup. His kisses nibbled downward, around my ear to the upper corner of my jaw. Though I tried to hold it in, he must have heard my gasp. His lips walked a wobbly line just below my jawbone, pulling at the weak flesh above my throat, working their way to my chin. I could not help but kiss his black satin locks. I took one curl between my teeth and clenched it as if I might suck from it not only his comfort but his strength as well. I needed strength. I felt myself at the edge of a dark abyss.

I had my clothes on but felt naked under his hands. They slid over my skin, skated through my flesh, dug at me, stroked me, yes he pawed me, he manhandled me, I was meat to his fingers, a toy to his hands, I did not care, no, no, not only did I not care, I wanted it, all of it, hot and strong and heaving, his power and urgency. Beyond self-control, I found myself eating at his head, my ravenous lips trying to take him inside me. I wanted his curly hair, his tight, round ears, the meat of his jaw, the tenderness of his cheek. I licked his eyes. I rubbed my whole face across his nose, letting it prod and tease my skin.

His hand went down the back of my pants like a ten snakes seeking dark shelter. I did not want him to go any further, but my will to resist hardly measured up to his longing. I think I heard him whimper, or maybe I just felt it. He had the side of his face pressed to my breast. He just rubbed and rubbed, as if he needed suckle. I wanted so much to give it to him. I pictured Kit seeing me. I imagined his disappointment, his sadness. I don't think he would have been angry. He would not have hated me or attacked the poor boy. He would have understood, but in sadness, and I would never want to make Kit sad, not even in his death.

He was tugging gently at my nipple when I finally tried to lift him away. But he would not part from me. He could not stop. When I pleaded, "Não, não, por favor... oh, please... please..." he merely burrowed his face deeper into me. My pleading was admittedly weak, and even as he lifted me from below, with one strong hand, I could not offer sufficient struggle. Depositing me in the hammock, he invaded me with absolute passion. My tummy heaved and jittered as he licked and chewed at it, his hand groping under my shirt to jostle my breasts, left and right, so eager with need. My moans of no, no, no carried undeniable undertones of yes, yes, yes. Yes and no. I didn't know what I wanted. I wanted him to stop; I wanted him to take me totally, in any way he wanted. I don't think I wanted any choice about it. I just wanted. I wanted. My pores exuded the sweat of my wanting. My words would make no difference. We had left the realm of words, rules, reason and control. We wanted, both of us. We wanted each other as much as anyone ever wanted food, water, air. We had become each other's necessity. When his lips and fingers began fumbling at the snap and zipper of my shorts, my hand of resistance came as weakly as a caress. He paused only to suck a chosen finger and then the one next to it, and then my pinky. I was then powerless beneath him, helpless. The hammock swung freely as he mounted it. I felt myself floating as if in air, and thus it was all the more shocking, even painful, when the door slammed open and the harsh yellow light of kerosene flame exploded into the room.

Rodrigo, his white shirt stained with a swath of perspiration, filled the doorway. The other room was astoundingly silent. The boy, my near-lover, leaped away from the hammock, coming to a strong, spread-leg stance. Rodrigo had something in his hand, a branch, I thought at first, but it wasn't. It was a rifle, a carbine with a clip not much bigger than a cigarette pack.

I couldn't understand what he growled at the boy, but the boy barked back at him with the kind of courage that gets men killed. Rodrigo argued back. I had no idea what the issue was, but I was pretty sure it was me. When Rodrigo gestured for the boy to get out, the boy said nothing. Rodrigo stepped aside, and the boy left, mad but peaceful.

Then Rodrigo glared at me, more or less pointed at me with the fist that held the rifle. "You," he sneered. "Come with me."

He noticed me snapping my pants shut, and as I passed him, his hand touched me at the waist to guide me through the door. The men in the other room watched in silence as Rodrigo and I walked out.

With his chin he motioned for me to go ahead, up the narrow board walkway to his hut – the one with the refrigerator and the medicine. It glowed dimly with kerosene light a hundred yards ahead. As he walked behind me, I imagined the key in the darkness of his pocket. He was wearing jeans. That meant four possible pockets, maybe even five. How was I going to get in there and get the key and then get the refrigerator open and then get some gasoline and then get into the canoe and then get away unnoticed. It was a lot of getting, and as far as I could tell, I was only getting into deeper danger.

My father taught me how to take a man down with any of various quick moves. If Rodrigo made the mistake of putting down his rifle and leaving himself vulnerable, I could kick downward against his knee or punch him in the groin or perhaps crack an ankle with a hard twist of the foot. But I doubted I could put him out of commission long enough to search his pockets. It wouldn't help to just make him mad.

But as I stepped into his hut, I noted that he leaned his carbine next to the door. I tried to see if it had a safety or some sign of whether it already had a round in the chamber. Not that I had any intentions of shooting him. But just in case.

Six feet away was the little refrigerator. S strong man could have lifted the thing right off the ground. The lock was indeed the kind that needed a key. The chain was very heavy duty.

He hadn't spoken a word to me, and he still didn't see any need to speak. With a tilt of his head he indicated his hammock. He didn't look happy, excited, impassioned or anything else. Just slightly bored and maybe a bit pissed off. At last he said a word, just a grunt, really. It barely fit through his tight lips. "Vamos," he said. Let's go.

"Rodrigo...I..."

But I had no words. I knew they would not affect him. There was no negotiating. His hand snaked over to my chin and lifted it so I faced his bored and bleary eyes. He tugged me toward him and leaned down a bit to put his lips to mine. I can't express the disgust I felt. It would have been a good moment to press my hands to his pockets, at least find the key, but he would have liked it too much. I just didn't want to show any cooperation at all. If he was going to screw me, I was going to make it clear that it was rape.

He raised me off the floor as if uprooting a tree. His cruel smile pressed in so close I could smell it. It smelled of whiskey, a rich-man's drink, not the cachaça of the poor. "Vamos fazer amor," he said in a sickening, sleazy voice. Let's make love.

It isn't making love when you have no choice. Granted, the puckish boy in the nightclub hadn't given me much choice, either, but he had swept up my desire. Rodrigo had just swept up my body, and that was all he was going to get – or even less if I could help it.

He lugged me over to the hammock and toppled forward to place me in it, himself atop. He squirmed around and did his best to get his tongue into my mouth. I did my best to keep it out. He seemed to enjoy the struggle of it. When I saw that part of the struggle was to keep my arms pinned down, I struggled a little more strategically, working my hands toward his pockets. He no doubt thought it accidental or just good luck. He was still smiling.

I felt it. My left hand felt it in his right pocket. I was just about to slip my fingers in there when I heard a thud, and Rodrigo suddenly went limp. I strained to look up around his head. There stood my puckish lover, the carbine in two hands. He had just smashed the butt of it into the back of Rodrigo's head.

"Vamos," he said.

I rolled Rodrigo off me and let him tumble to the dirt floor. The boy held the carbine on him as he reached down to me. But before I took his hand I fished the key from Rodrigo's pocket.

I explained nothing as I rushed to the refrigerator and fiddled with the lock. As soon as it clicked open I threw off the chain and yanked open the door.

There was no medicine. Not a bit. All I found was a handful of sand in a metal dish. By the time I recognized it, young Puck was on his knees beside me. He lifted the dish as if it held a sacred substance – and indeed it did. It was gold, the product of several days' mining.

His eyes gleamed with gold as his fingers lightly brushed the dust, then pinched up a bit to feel its texture.

"Leave it," I said. "Gold is death." I didn't mean to sound so profound. The words just appeared in my mouth. As I spoke them, I remembered Ronsh and his dying tribe.

"Where's the medicine?"

"The what?"

He looked completely incredulous that I could ask about something in the presence of so much gold. The pile in the tray must have weighed a couple of pounds. It was probably worth more than he'd earn in his entire lifetime.

"The medicine."

He snorted with disdain. "Yes, it was here. But Rodrigo sold it. He keeps some for himself and lets his workers die. And of course the gold stays with him." His eyes gleamed even more fiercely. "But no more;."

With the tray of gold in one hand, he used the other to aim the rifle at Rodrigo, who still lay motionless in the dirt. "No more," he said.

I said, "No!" and pushed the rifle away. "If you shoot, other men come."

The boy hesitated and apparently came to the same conclusion. He looked around quickly, grabbed a sheet of old newspaper from a stack in the corner, opened a page, dumped the gold in the middle, folded up a neat little package, wedged it down the front of his shorts and said, "OK, vamos."

We slipped out and headed down the wooden walkway toward the river. I was surprised to see the sky already turning rosy with the first signs of dawn. Long white clouds reached across the sky like skeleton fingers, and monstrous dark-blue thunderhead loomed in the distance. I wondered where Soong Tan was and where she'd slept and what she was doing. I had a sneaking suspicion she wasn't sitting under a tree reading a book. Somehow I just knew.

Why was I not surprised to find Elsi down by the river? She was lying on a plank of wood, just waking up. She'd slept there all night, I could tell, probably to escape the heat of her fever. My fellow escapee said nothing when I gestured for her to get into the canoe. "Vamos," I said to her. "We're going away."

She asked no questions. She just got in the middle of the canoe and sat into the puddle in the bottom. I sat on the seat in the front. The boy started the little motor. It caught on the second pull of the rope. With a foot in the river he shoved us off. The sound of that motor pushing us downstream and away from that place was one of the sweetest sounds I've ever heard.

Once we rounded a bend, something occurred to me. I turned in my seat and shouted back, "The medicine...where did Rodrigo sell it?" I mean, where the hell do you sell medicine in the middle of the jungle?

"Madeireiros," he shouted. I had to think about it. It sounded like the word for wood. I repeated the word so I wouldn't forget it.

"Where are they?" I asked, hoping that might give me a clue.

Without a word he pointed upstream. I still had no idea what he meant, and suddenly it didn't matter. The motor sputtered, coughed, shuddered and died. After a brief wash of water at the bow, we floated in silence. It was as terrifying as a hand around the throat.

The kid started paddling with our only paddle. The current helped. But it wasn't long before we heard the whine of a motor half a mile back upstream.

The boy paddled hard for the bank. I crouched at the bow, reaching to grab the first piece of vegetation I could. Leaves came off in my hand. We drifted downstream. I grabbed at a branch, held tight. The canoe kept drifting. I pulled hard, stopping the canoe and gradually pulling us in. But just as I had a good grip on it underneath me, it snapped. I tumbled face-first into the lukewarm water. When I came up, I saw the canoe drifting away as my boy paddled furiously to turn it around and come back for me. It was a complicated maneuver that forced him to turn away from the bushes on the bank and out into the current. I held onto the branch and struggled to gain some kind of footing. I was terrified that I'd step on an alligator or something. I was just reaching for the canoe when I heard the crack of a rifle and the instant blip of water just a few feet away. The boy made a quick decision. It shocked me at first, but I knew he was right. He pointed into the forest and shouted, "Go!"

He gave me no choice. He turned and paddled furiously downstream. A couple more gunshots missed him. He fired a couple of quick shots back at them as the canoe drifted farther downstream. Having achieved nothing with that, he started paddling hard, throwing up wide splashes of green-brown water. By the time I pulled myself up onto semi-solid ground, he was around the bend.

The oncoming canoe now had to make a choice – me or the boy. At least one of us would escape. In the river, it would be their motorized canoe against his paddle. On land, it would be my feet against theirs. I can jog five miles without problem. I doubted they could. I was glad when I saw them head for me.

The vegetation was very dense for a good hundred feet. I wasn't running as much as wrestling through vines and branches. My soaked clothes weighed like lead. Behind me, men shouted and growled as they stumbled through the rough tunnel I had opened for them. With a sudden explosion of sweat, I realized that they had a clear advantage. They also had a gun. I had to not only stay ahead of them but beyond sight.

I wanted to stop and pray when the vegetation thinned out and opened into clear forest floor. I broke into a hard run, not in a straight line – I couldn't – but dodging trees, staying low, putting distance between me and them. A shot, not as far away as I'd hoped, sent a bullet ticking through the leaves to my right. They were keeping up.

I had vague intentions of more or less following the river and perhaps meeting up with the canoe, but I was running pretty much blind. The ground was rising. Soon I was scrambling uphill on all fours, pulling at roots and branches to keep from falling back. They were right on me. I was in plain sight. When a shot twacked into the ground just a few inches from my hand, I expected the next through the back of my skull. I did not want to die that way, deep in the jungle, no one ever knowing what happened to me, and Soong Tan waiting, waiting, waiting until...I don't know what. I kept struggling upward and with my last bit of strength reached the top of the ridge. I was quite surprised to find a trail there.

It was narrow and no doubt made by animals. Branches that crossed it were just two or three feet above the ground. I became an animal myself, scurrying along, my hands keeping my chest off the ground, my legs propelling me forward like a dog.

And still the men came behind me. My lungs were burning. My arm muscles were collapsing under my weight. If I'd had time to stop, I would have peeled off my wet clothes. They seemed to hold me back like a net. The thunderhead I'd seen earlier devoured the sun, leaving the forest floor in eerie semi-darkness. I practically slid head-first when the trail turned downward. Gravity was of no help. Descending only tired my legs more. I was entering denser forest, trees that rose into a dark-green sky of leaves. The deeper in I ran, the darker it got. It was a place to die. I felt that inside. I felt as if I were already underground.

The trail wound around trees as thick as houses, past massive roots that rose up to form trunks. I could not see the men behind me, but I could hear their feet pounding the forest floor. When I came to trail crossing the one I was on, I saw a chance at life – one chance in three. If I chose the trail they didn't, I might live.

I had neither time to think, no reason to turn one way or the other. I turned left, but in my weakness I must have left marks. They followed. I was no longer running, just stumbling, just reaching for a few extra feet before I collapsed. I cannot find words to describe how I felt when I came around the base of a tree and looked up to see an Indian squatting in the branches, all but naked, painted in stripes like an animal, a bow stretched out, a long arrow pointed right at me, and a little face, like a little girl's, a panther-girl with jaguar hair and eyes the color of jungle, a little mouth agape with incomprehension. I stumbled forward, using the last of my strength to keep from falling too hard, reaching out as if to the feet of a god. The Indian's voice shot out as shrill as the cry of a bird, and I obeyed even before I understood it as English, plain and beautiful, tinged with a hint of Burmese. It said, "Drop!"

And I dropped. I skidded forward into the dirt. The arrow whistled over me with the softness of a mourning dove. Though my face was pressed to the humid earth, I heard the arrow hit meat and the meat hit the ground. Then another arrow whistled by, hit meat, produced a scream of pain. I just held onto the ground, digging into it with my fingers as if I might fall away. More arrows whistled by, a storm of arrows flying in from different angles and distances, deadly angels flying in to save me. I just lay there crying into the earth and holding on until small hands reached around my face, little lips pressed to my cheek, and tiny tears fell down to touch my own.

Chapter Nineteen

War

The little hunters could hardly believe what they had done. Two men lay dead in the trail. Two others had limped off, wounded, doomed to die of the toad poison the arrows had injected into their bloodstreams. The children had not meant to kill, but when they saw Soong Tan let loose an arrow, and then another, they did as she had done. Then, in a circle, they watched as Soong Tan lifted Ysa's head from the earth as if raising her back from a grave. Ysa did not understand what Soong Tan said to her friends, but it must have been good. They all squatted around her and put their little brown hands on her. They chanted something. Ysa's energy returned. She felt as light as an angel.

They led her back to the Indian village. Ronsh showed no surprise when she emerged from the forest and follow the line of little warriors through the patch of manioc. He was out there with a shovel, digging up manioc tubers, the main staple of Indians. But as she drew nearer, she saw that he had already dug much deeper than tubers. The blade of his short-handled shovel, rusty near the handle, silvery at the edge, was worn almost in half. It was probably the only shovel the village had. Beside the hole was a flame-colored hammock wrapped around something lumpy. Manioc, Ysa thought at first, but then she realized it was a body. Ronsh was digging a grave.

It was not the first grave among the manioc. A wide area she had assumed cleared for harvest was actually checkered with fresh graves. It was hard to tell where one grave ended and the next began. They hadn't been dug in neat rows. She guessed they had been dug where the manioc looked ripe

Ronsh stopped shoveling only long enough to look up at her empty hands. He did not need to say anything.

"The medicine is not there," Ysa said. "It is with the *madeireiros*. Who are they?"

Ronsh did not look at her, did not respond to her excuse or answer her question. He just kept lifting small mounds of sandy clay from the bottom of the hole and heaving it up onto a sloppy pile. Ysa said nothing more. It was his turn to speak. He was in no hurry to move on to a decision.

He stopped digging, not when he reached some appropriate depth but when he lacked the energy to dig more. He glistened with sweat. His exhaustion weighed heavily on his arms. Still not speaking, he climbed from the hole and lifted one end of the hammock. With his eyes he asked Ysa to get the other end. They didn't lift it so much as drag the weight of the corpse to edge of grave, then lower it in. As it lowered, it opened a bit. Ronsh's mother lay inside, curled up, almost fetal, almost as if asleep.

With heavy tenderness, he tucked the hammock around her, then came up to shovel in the dirt. Ysa watched his eyes. He did not cry. If the eyes are the windows to the soul, His soul was absent, traveling far away on a trip where it had never been.

After he had replaced all the dirt he had removed, he stuck the shovel in the ground, crossed his arms over his chest and looked at Ysa.

"You were right," he said.

She resisted the urge to blurt, Who, me? She did not know what he meant. She tried to remember what she might have told him. How could she possibly have been right about anything? She'd done nothing but screw up since she'd arrived.

Finally he spoke, but he did not look at her. He was speaking to the darkened earth of his mother's grave. "The Indian's problem," he said, "is the White Man. It is civilization. We cannot live with it. It cannot help us. It only kills us."

She followed him as he walked back to center of the village. He left the shovel near the grave site. His words were ominous. He had concluded something more than the fact that Indians had to solve their own problem. He had a solution in mind. It would not come easily.

"The *madeireiros* are the men who cut our trees," he said. "They come with motor-saws and guns. They kill everything. They are a disease in the forest. The miners kill the water. The *madeireiros* kill the forest. Without water and forest, the Indians die. For centuries we have died of disease and hunger – deaths of weakness. For centuries we waited for the problem to go away. We listened to lies and believed them because it was easier to believe than to act. We believed that civilization would share its good things with us. But all it shares is disease and hunger and greed."

"So...what are you going to do?"

"We are going to take control of our land and our lives. We will cut ourselves off from your uncivilized world. We will begin with the *madeireiros*. We will do to them what they have done to our forest. We will destroy their boats, burn their camp, take their medicine, cut them down like trees and leave their souls to God." Ronsh smiled. "We will let the forest have them. It is just, no? Beautifully just."

"But...who will do this? The children? Where are your men?"

"Our few men left the village to escape the sickness. I have sent for them to return. We will invite others from other tribes. All Indians are brothers. We all know what we must do to survive. It will begin now. And you will be part of it.

At just about the time Ysa was becoming involuntary chief medical officer for the greatest Indian uprising since the eighteenth century, Edgar, Gumball King of Amazonia, was paddling up to the logging camp with Elizama in an inflatable raft. Its oars looked no bigger than ice cream scoops. They'd landed the plane somewhere upstream. Their gumball machine had arrived like some kind of god floating down from the sky. Now Edgar was coming in to capitalize on the dramatic entrance.

Just Kit was surprised to see a gumball machine arriving from out of the blue, Edgar was every bit as surprised to find Kit at the logging camp. Not just Kit but Kit in chains. And not just Kit in chains but Gaia, too – Gaia half naked in her camouflage panties and still tied to the log at the sawmill, the blade, now stopped, just inches from her waist. She had gone catatonic, quivering with fear, gushing with tears, blubbering with maniacal pleas and prayers to everybody from heaven to hell and all points in between.

Kit was cool. As Edgar arrived, Kit was demonstrating his mastery of gumball technology. Naturally the loggers had no idea what the damned thing was. They were just about to decapitate it with a machete when Kit stopped them and showed them the power of a twenty-five-centavo coin. The pinwheel spun, sparks flew, the siren wailed, a brilliant blue sphere rolled around and around and around the spiral chute, and...presto! A big blue gumball! He let them pass it around like some kind of extra-terrestrial diamond. They examined it the way a pack of monkeys would, squinting at it, sniffing it, clicking it against their teeth, scratching it with their thumbnails, grunting.

"Gum!" Kit said when it found its way back to his magical gringo hands. "Watch!" He popped it into his mouth and chewed for his life. They didn't exactly ooo and ah over that. They already understood the concept of chewing gum. They'd just never seen it in the form of a blue ball, let alone from such a machine that looked like it might be distantly related to an atomic weapon.

He chewed like crazy until it had the proper consistency for blowing a bubble. With all due theatricality, he inflated a doozy, held his hands out like a Flying Wallenda on a high-wire, and begged up a little round of applause led off by Edgar and Elizama.

"*Muito bom, muito bom!*" Edgar said, clapping and stepping into the circle to stand at Kit's side.

As Edgar faced the audience, Kit whispered, "You'd better find a way to get us the hell out of here, brother. These are not the friendliest of natives."

Edgar appeared not to hear. He was addressing the loggers as if he were the Pope, they the humble peasants of the Holy Roman Empire.

"*Senhores*," he sang, "I present to you the most magnificent recreational snack food vending system ever to be found in the great forest of Amazonia! Into your dreary lives comes the option to clean your teeth, exercise your jaw, prevent cavities, eliminate intestinal ailments, discourage headaches, soothe the pains and itches of venereal disease, retard the aging process and infuse the muscles and brain with the natural energy of sugar that was grown and processed in the great nation of Brazil! All this for only twenty-five centavos! Just watch the beauty of this North American technology in action..."

With that, he help up a coin for all to see, showed them both sides of it, slipped it into the slot, and gave the crank a smooth twirl. The pinwheel spun, sparks flew, the siren wailed, a bright red gumball rolled around and around and around the spiral chute, and presto! – Edgar held it up for all to see. When he tossed it into the air, it did not produce the expected riot. One man reached up and captured it into a fist. It was Big Boss Leon, and he didn't look happy.

Who could blame him? His men were supposed to be cutting down the rain forest, not lusting after gum. On top of that, his little game with Gaia had gotten more complex. Now another gringo, and his daffy-looking woman, had entered the scene. He hadn't forgotten the purple porpoises. The whole situation looked undeniably suspicious. For all he knew, American satellites were gazing down on them, the Polícia Militar were on their way, and Greenpeace had the place surrounded. Either that or the winds of fate had blown him four nitwits and a gumball machine.

He kept his fist in the air as he growled, "Tell me why you are here." His eyes were scrunched into black knots.

Edgar's eyes lit up with the enthusiasm of a salesman confronting a hot prospect. "And you, my good man, must be the chief of this enterprise?"

"Maybe," he said in clipped Portuguese.

"Please...keep the gum. A gift to you from the great leader of my country." Edgar beamed with pride and beneficence.

The man's expression did not change a bit as he unwrapped his fist from the gumball and tossed it away. Edgar shifted a bit toward seriousness but continued his pitch.

"I see we have much to discuss," he said. "This is good. Please allow me to present myself: Edgar Entwhistle, Brazilian-American Enterprises." He marched forward to force Leon into a handshake. Kit marveled at his foster-brother's tactical astuteness. Within two minutes he had developed an initial rapport with the man. Now, at least, they could negotiate. That was more than Kit had accomplished in almost three days.

The Big Boss said nothing. Edgar, sensing the need to keep things rolling, filled the silence with more words. Kit wondered how he could think of so much to say. He also wondered how long Edgar could keep it up before he stuck his foot in his mouth and got everybody killed. He entertained himself with an image of Edgar in a coffin, one leg halfway down his throat and a wad of green gum stuffed up his nose.

Edgar leaned in close to the Bossman. His arm sneaked across the Bossman's shoulders, disguised as a buddy-buddy back-slap but evolving into a one-armed embrace. With his other hand, Edgar illustrated the features of the gumball machine and the benefits of owning one. Kit could almost read Edgar's lips as he went through his spiel about profit margins, employee morale, ergonometric decors, the history and traditions of gum-chewing since the times of the ancient Egyptians. Edgar's hand rose high to evoke the grandeur of the pyramids, then swooped in low to touch Leon just over his heart.

The Boss nodded with tentative agreement. Edgar, guiding his prey by the shoulders, moved him toward the shack which Gaia had so recently visited. Elizama followed a few feet behind, looking around as if on a tour.

The other men stayed around the gumball machine as if it might bolt off into the jungle and escape. Kit would have liked to do the same. Given Edgar's apparent success thus far, however, he thought it best to sit tight. Not that he had much choice. He was just worried about the deal Edgar might be working out with the Big Boss. Was he trading logs for the gumball machine? Or people for gumballs? Was Gaia included? And how were the four of them going to get away in an inflatable raft barely big enough for two?

The discussions inside the Boss's shack went on for a long, long time. Elizama waited outside. Kit postponed any thought, schemes or plans until he knew what Edgar was up to. He just sat under his tree, sweating and working his fingers under the chain that itched and pinched his neck. It itched and hurt. In a curious development, Edgar leaned out of the shack to talk with Elizama. She then went over to Gaia and spoke with her for a moment. Then she returned to the shack and spoke with Edgar.

Soon Edgar and the Boss came out of the shack. They went out of sight around back. Incredibly, they returned with a rustic coffin, deep but ridiculously short, unvarnished but streaked with tar along the seams between the slats. Kit didn't like the looks of it. It was the right size for a fat child or an adult who had been, say, sawed in half. Like some kind of death-porter, Edgar carried it on his head. Elizama carried a folding beach chair. Leon lugged a log stool. At The Boss's instruction, a worker hurried over to Gaia, untied her from her death log and dragged her to Kit's tree. She stumbled as she came, trying to hold one arm across her tiny, naked breasts.

Edgar delivered the news with utter glee. "Kit, my man, my brother," he gushed, "you won't believe what I've learned."

Kit was fairly sure Edgar was right: There would be no believing this one. He said, "Break it to me gently, Edgar."

Edgar set the coffin in the shade of the Kit's tree and adjusted it to a secure position. "Our friend of the great woods here," Edgar said, "it turns out he plays bridge."

"*Bridge?*"

Edgar produced a deck of cards from the interior of his safari vest and repeated the unbelievable truth: "Bridge."

"Bridge."

"Don't play dumb, brother-o-mine. Bridge."

"North, east, south, west, bidding, rubbers, tricks, trump, all that stuff?"

"Right. Bridge."

"Like we used to play? In the cafeteria in high school?"

Edgar's eyes fastened hard onto Kit's. The pause between the question and the answer was discernible only to boys who had grown up together. His voice as flat as Kansas, Edgar just said, "Yes," and Kit knew exactly what he meant.

He meant bridge á la Edgar, a bridge so dirty it made the Brooklyn Bridge look like something you could eat off. Bridge dealt off the bottom, bridge with secret signals, footsie and winks, sniffs and coughs, Morse code tapped out with nervous fingers, a bridge unbeatable and undetectable by any but the most professional observer.

"What's with the coffin?" Kit asked, expecting the worst.

"Unless you brought a card table, this is what we've got. Our friend Leon's been dying – so to speak – to play bridge for months out here in his jungle retreat. But he can't find a fourth, let alone a third or second. So guess what we're going to do, you, me and Gaia."

"Get cut in half by pissed-off lumberjacks?"

"Not if we're lucky."

"Since when did you depend on luck to win anything?"

Edgar shot him a hard look of mutual understanding. Kit understood it to mean shut up, stupid, and play along. But his voice remained jovial and excited. "Have a seat, foster-bro," he said. "Does your chain reach far enough or should we slide this coffin your way?"

Big Boss Leon set the log stool to Edgar's right and a made gracious gesture for the half-naked Gaia to sit. Then he signaled for one of his men to fetch a couple of crates.

"And could we get a shirt for this girl?" Edgar suggested. "I can't concentrate in a topless situation."

With a tilt of his head, Leon sent a man to fetch Gaia's T-shirt.

Edgar explained that Kit was to be his partner. Gaia would play with Leon. They would play by the Queen's rules. One rubber, winner takes all.

Kit eyed Edgar suspiciously. "All what?"

"Freedom," Edgar said, suddenly dead serious.

Gaia gasped and seemed incapable of exhalation. Leon looked at all of them through one squinted eye.

Edgar said, "Exciting, isn't it?"

"Couldn't we have been consulted about this before we sat down at the table?" Kit asked.

"But how does it work?" Gaia asked. "Who gets to go free?"

"If you and Mr. Leon win, you go free," Edgar explained. "Kit, however, would be thrown to the lions. I understand the men here are quite upset. Some property was damaged. Some teeth were kicked out. I'm sure we can all sympathize with their feelings and understand their claim that some retribution is called for."

"They were going to cut me up with a chain saw," Kit snarled.

"As their supervisor has explained it to me, you had trespassed into one of their trees and were subsequently employed as their prisoner, which, of course, gave them the right to saw you up or engage in whatever leisure time activity met their hearts' content."

"Yeah, but..."

Leon spoke up with a very prissy British accent. "This isn't London, you know."

Kit withdrew to his former cool. Edgar was joking around, but the situation was real. If they lost the rubber, he was food for flies.

If, however, he and Edgar won, Gaia would become the loggers' toy – a fate worse than getting sawed in half.

So purple porpoises were no longer the problem. Gaia was no longer concerned with the slaughter of trees. Her eyes met Kit's. Neither of them had words for their feelings. Kit wondered how hard Gaia was going to play to protect herself. He could not blame her for her instinct to survive. He expected it of her. He wished he could tell her that. But then it occurred to him that he could easily throw the game her way. A stupid move or two, an excessive bid, a failure to pick up Edgar's signals. In other words, it wasn't her choice; it was his. He could make the game go either way.

The question was: would he try to win or try to lose?

He did not know the answer. His decision, then, was pure Kit. As I once heard him say, When you have no answer, change the question. Don't play by their rules for their stakes. Think of something else.

He saw no easy solution. All he could do at that point was stall for time. He'd make the games last as long as he could. With a little luck – or a full-blown miracle – he'd think of a way out.

He held his hand to Gaia. She touched it lightly. "Play well," he said. "I wish you to win....I love you."

She did not reply.

Edgar snapped the cards in a quick, hard shuffle. "I can see this is going to be a most interesting game," he said. "I hope we can count on everyone to play his or her best."

The game would be interesting for him. No matter who won, he would walk away – or paddle away. He and Elizama would leave with either Gaia or Kit. Kit honestly wondered which his foster brother wanted. He sure loved his money, and if he was any kind of healthy male, he wouldn't mind sharing a little inflatable boat with a girl in camouflage panties. His flip, carefree attitude just didn't ring right. Now he would be controlling the game with his tricks and signals. Could he be trusted? If so, why had he set up this stupid game in the first place? He had an ulterior motive. Kit was sure of it.

But Edgar's motives didn't matter. The outcome of the rubber didn't matter. Not as long as Kit thought of some way out. He didn't have much time. The first team to win three hands won the rubber. But it didn't matter who won. That was Kit's attitude.

Edgar shuffled. Leon cut. Kit took up the deck to deal. As Elizama draped herself over her husband's shoulder, Edgar suddenly snapped his fingers and reached inside his vest. Before his hand came out, six small caliber weapons were aimed at his chest. He brought his hand out very slowly and slowly opened it to reveal several coins. He handed them to one of the men and gestured toward the gumball machine. "Gentlemen, the gum's on me."

That little distraction gave Kit plenty of time to check the ace of clubs on the bottom of the deck. Once he knew what trump would be, the bidding was easy. Gaia, chewing on her pinky, suggested hearts. Edgar upped her by a spade. Leon went to two diamonds. Kit went to three clubs. Edgar pushed it to four.

"That settles it," Edgar said to Kit. "Clubs are trump, you're dummy and I'm driving this death machine."

"And I'm glad of it," Kit added. H leaned back to watch his fate unfold. He was somewhat relieved not to have to be thinking about the game. It was hard enough to win at bridge without worrying about whether you want to win.

So he sat back and enjoyed it. It was like old times, back in the John Jay High School cafeteria. By all appearances, it was only through sheer brilliance that Leon and Gaia headed off disaster by taking -- tricks. Edgar cursed and slammed the coffin-table every time he lost a trick. Kit snapped at him as if angry. Edgar snapped back. Leon glowed with satisfaction. Gaia sniffled, torn between crying with fear and giggling at the horrific absurdity of playing bridge for her life in camouflage panties under a lone tree in what used to be a forest.

Leon dealt the next round. Kit couldn't shuffle like he used to. Neither he nor Edgar got an ace, and Gaia, quite accidentally it seemed, took trump. Kit doubted that Edgar had planned for her to win that hand, but she did. She made it look as if just dumb luck killed trick after trick. Tears kept oozing from her face, but she kept making the right decisions. She made her bid.

"Oh, God," she prayed, clasping he hands and looking up toward heaven. "Oh, God."

"I didn't know you were a believer," Kit said.

"I wasn't," she squeaked. "Now I am." She closed her eyes and murmured words of thanks to He Who had tilted the game in her favor.

Now Kit was worried. Either there was a God of Bridge or Gaia and Leon were secret champs, or Edgar was trying to lose. It couldn't possibly have been just luck. Edgar didn't play by luck. He considered luck unfair. Kit remembered what he'd always said when they were kids: "What fun is a game of luck? Why go through the motions? Cheating is skill. That's what makes the game interesting."

It was weird to cheat under the gaze of a dozen people, most of them armed, all of them working over superwads of gum as they tried to figure out the rules of the game. None of the onlookers had any idea why Edgar held his pinky at such an odd, crooked angle, why Kit picked his left nostril with his longest finger, why Edgar burped and wiped his forehead, why Kit shook his head only from center to left. By the time Leon nailed down trump at three spades, Kit knew Edgar's hand exactly. Leon failed to make his bid, and Gaia shot Kit a dirty look. She seemed to suspect that she had been betrayed, and not by her newfound God.

Three hands wins a rubber. Kit and Edgar had one, Bossman Leon and Fruitcake Gaia already had two. So when Kit won the next round of bidding, he had to take the hand. And he did. Not that it was hard. Edgar had dealt him a hand as nearly perfect as anyone could believe.

They played the final round. Gaia was dummy and Leon was trying for three clubs. The cards came down as if foreordained, and when the last card of the last trick hit the table, it caught Kit by surprise. The end had come suddenly, a quick several rounds of cards, hand over fist, and it was over. He had thought of nothing, no alternative to the cruel and absurd agreement Edgar had worked out with Leon. A simple eight of hearts cinched the rubber for Edgar and Kit.

So Gaia would be the sacrificial lamb. Utter silence swallowed the end of the game. No one moved except to look at Gaia. Edgar looked oddly satisfied. Kit, his heart sending full-bodied throbs through his arteries, just wanted to reach out to her, to take her into his arms, to somehow protect her and even just feel her warmth. He loved her in a certain way, the way of the survivors of trauma, the way of people who share a secret, who have been through experiences no one else could even imagine. That kind of love is as "true" as anything two teenage lovers ever felt. He and Gaia were about as close as two people can get without going through a few decades of marriage. As soon as she became the loser, he fervently wished it were him.

Big Leon's left eyeball was raping Gaia in the silence. His right eye was tucked into a knot of eyelash so tight it looked like a place death might hide. Kit thought maybe he'd lash him with a backswung fist, maybe break his jaw and a few teeth. But that wouldn't have helped at all, not so long as he was still chained at the neck and surrounded by thugs who all but dripped with a common desire to get their hands on Leon's leftovers.

It was Edgar who interrupted the silence ."Well," he said, not uncheerfully, "perhaps someone might be interested in a little game of poker." He rapped the coffin with optimistic enthusiasm.

Maybe Leon just liked cards. He wasn't satisfied with winning a human being, fair and square – more than fair and square, when you think about it. He'd won by losing. He had Gaia instead of Kit, tender baby veal instead of bear gristle. He'd probably wanted her all along.

The four of them worked out the bizarre game of poker ever played on the face of the earth. Edgar set the terms, apparently making them as complicated as possible: Five card draw, full deck, two draws with second draw only with a face card retained, a pair or better to open. One eyed jacks were wild. Aces high and low.

The rules weren't the only weird part of this game. The betting was even more bizarre. They anted with cash. Edgar coughed it up for Kit; Leon coughed it for his slave, Gaia. From there, however, it started to look like a yard sale. Leon bet a chain saw. Edgar matched it with his watch, a solid gold Timex. With twelve genuine diamonds and leatherette strap. Kit and Gaia folded right then and there. Edgar lost his watch to three kings.

They played hand after hand, laying a laughable assortment of goods on the table. Edgar won a quart of chain saw oil. Kit won Leon's coffin-table and the saw that had almost cut him in half. Leon wasn't worried about the loss of the coffin.

"You can have it," he said, waving away an invisible nothing. "We've got all the coffins for which a person could wish."

"What do you do?" Edgar asked. "Collect them?"

Leon tittered like a British lord. "Very good, very good," he said. "No, coffins are a side business for us. When a tree does not meet export standards, we saw it up and make coffins. They're especially popular at the gold mines."

As they played, Kit just couldn't get a read on Leon's face. It seemed to be playing some other game in some other place. Edgar put on his jovial, devil-may-care poker face which in a college dorm would have passed for drunkenness. No matter what her hand, Gaia looked like she had a foot caught in a bear trap. She went through the motions of assembling a hand, but she always folded right away. After all, what could she possibly gain? A chain saw? A watch? The only time she stayed in was when Leon bet her shirt. He owned it, right? So in a gesture of cruelty, he had her add it to the kitty. His loggers all but drooled.

"Absurdo!" Elizama yelped. "Here, leetle gerl, you bet my earhings." And she dropped the pair into the kitty. Gaia stayed in.

Kit, in pity, folded a pair of aces just to keep the betting from going higher.

Wen Edgar sang out, "I bet my wife's bra," she smacked him on the head. Leon let it slide. Thanks to a one-eyed jack, he had a straight. Gaia, left topless, now possessing nothing in the world besides army-issue underdrawers, refused to play anymore. She just lay her head on the table and wept. Kit tried to comfort her with a hand to the top of her head, but it had no effect.

After a few sad moments, Edgar announced, "Last hand," and set the cards in front of Leon for a cut.

I guess Edgar dealt well. The betting on the first draw went wild. It wasn't just the good hands that everybody had. It was because nobody wanted the junk they'd won earlier. What was Edgar going to do with a chain saw? Of what possible use would a coffin be? Who but Gaia needed her shirt?

But then it got serious. Edgar was no longer smiling. He said, "I raise it by one gumball machine."

Kit, having no such assets left, tossed in his full house. It was up to Leon to match gumball machine. Scrutinizing Edgar's face, then his own cards, then the back of Edgar's, then Edgar's face again, he said, "All right. I bet the bimbo. Am I correct in divining your objective? One card please." With painful reluctance, he peeled a card from his hand and laid it face down on the coffin.

"One card for the player," Edgar said, "and the dealer takes one, too."

Kit watched for Edgar's slick deal off the bottom of the deck, a move so polished that it had won him small fortunes in high school and larger fortunes in Nevada casinos. He did it well...except this time. Maybe it was the sweat dribbling down his fingers. Maybe it was the very high stakes. Maybe it was because Elizama chose that moment to smack a mosquito that had landed on Edgar's neck. Whatever the cause, it was clear where the card came from even before it flipped face up on the table, the ace of spades – the card of death.

The table exploded. Kit, seeing what was coming, leaped up to take a swing at Leon before he reached Edgar. Edgar, forgetting that he had bigger problems, practically pounced on Elizama, She just screamed, having no idea what had happened. Gaia recoiled in horror, covering herself with her arms as Leon's men drew weapons and reached for all four players for four different reasons. Kit managed to knock one down with a back-swing of his elbow, then to punch one in the jaw before something heavy came down on his head. Gaia, screaming, fell into half a dozen arms and hands that were only pretending to restrain her. Leon got his hands around Edgar's neck and gripped tight as several men pounded on Edgar.

Kit didn't see all that followed. He didn't gain consciousness until they threw him to the ground near the saw mill. Gaia landed on top of him. He seemed to awaken into a different world. A gargantuan cloud, truly black, rose up over the camp, swallowing the sun and all but a hint of light. Wind, springing up from the ground, lashed at the sea of dead branches. Dust and dead leaves rose into the air as if coming to life. Thunder threatened from the near distance, advancing by flashes and explosions. For a moment, Kit thought he was back in a Cambodian jungle, under attack by an unseen enemy in a smoke-blackened battlefield.

He couldn't see Edgar or Elizama. In fact he couldn't see much at all. His head felt as if a spear had shot him through the left eye, and his vision blurred with red. He recognized Gaia's hot body as it crashed onto him. Instinctively, he clung to her as a swimmer might cling to a log in the middle of the sea. Still, he forced himself to rise, to face his enemies on their own level. He pulled Gaia up with him, keeping her small, heaving breasts tight against his naked torso, unconsciously trying to pull her inside himself where she might be safe. When the mill started up, she buried her face in his chest and screamed, screamed, screamed. The big, round blade rotated slowly at first, as if awakening, just rumbling until it suddenly accelerated to a thin, high-pitched hum.

Twenty feet away, two men aimed rifles at them. Another prepared a log and some rope. Up by the tree, Leon and some other men were kicking Edgar around and shouting at him. Kit didn't know why, had absolutely no idea why, but the moment seemed right for a kiss – the kind of kiss that goes beyond love to reach the realm of life and death, a kiss of good-bye not to a lover but to life itself, life and all that is precious about it. Love is one of those precious things, love in all its infinite meanings and manifestations. Gaia pressed against him like hot putty. She whimpered with inexpressible emotion as her breath heaved in and out through her nose. Her lips dug at his mouth, desperately hungry for the unattainable. He hand quivered across the skin of his shoulder and her leg wrapped around him as if to climb up from earth, away from Hell. It was one of those kisses, deep, complex, visceral, from a place in the gut that few people know about. It took a long, long time yet could not possibly last long enough.

Chapter Twenty

Coffins: Small, Medium, Large

Ysa was as much a captive as Kit and in just about as much danger. She knew she was in trouble when the Indian men started drinking. It wasn't Bud Light. It was some kind of fermented stuff they sucked out of a big gourd. At least fifty men, braves, she supposed, had appeared in the village as if from nowhere, arriving on paths from various directions. They were all painted up and stripped down to little loin cloths made of something that looked like woven coconut threads. They looked grim, the way men look before they stand to face their deaths, and they drank as if receiving a sacrament.

Soong Tan, who was still painted up like a jungle bird, and Ysa stayed away. They kept to the landing at the river, near the canoe. It felt slightly safer there, away from the warriors and the disease. Ysa was fashioning a sling for her medical bag so she could carry it across her back. She knew they were in for a long hike.

"Are we really going to see a war?" Soong Tan asked. She sounded much more serious than the average eleven-year-old, as if she had already witnessed the frenzy of people slaughtering each other.

"I just hope we can stay out of it," Ysa said.

"Do I get to go?"

Ysa hesitated. Which would be safer, to leave her at the village, which might well fall under counterattack, or to stay at the fringe of the battlefield? Not sure exactly what she meant, she said, "You'll stay with me."

"Good."

Ronsh was among a growing band of warriors. She did not recognize him at first. He had shed his jeans and plaid shirt, painted his body with stripes that looked like colorful scars, and put on the simple loin cloth of his fellow warriors. With a change of clothes, he had abandoned the twentieth century and returned to Paleolithic times. Everyone else had done the same, and they were taking Ysa and Soong Tan with them. They were going to attack the twentieth century, and Ysa was half confident they would win. She was equally sure they would lose.

They did not offer their brew to Ysa. It was obviously a ceremony of men only. They kept to themselves, squatting between a hut and the manioc field. The women of the village stayed away. They looked even more worried than the men. Once in a while a woman, almost in tears, would shout something over to the men, and one of the men would shout something back. The tone of it sounded a lot like shut up/don't bother me.

"They're getting stinking drunk," Ysa said, only vaguely aware that it was little Soong Tan who would hear.

"It makes them brave," she said. "The kids told me about it. They think it protects them from death, that it cures everything."

on Wall Street, in Geneva, in Tokyo. They had never seen the rain forest. They had no idea how human beings lived there, how the invasion of civilization sickened, killed and destroyed. The people about to die on both sides of this Indian war were on the front line, as it were, only for their need to survive.

The real question, she knew, was one of perception. Did the Indians really perceive her as being on their side? Or did they see her as their captive, a white woman whose true loyalty was with the White Men, so-called civilization, the loggers and gold miners, the bankers and merchants and politicians?

How would the loggers perceive her? As an Indian sympathizer? A traitor to the cause of civilization and profit?

She was scared. She knew that the Indians did not see her as an one of them, and the loggers would not see her as one of them. The irony saddened her. Both perceptions were false. All she wanted to do was find her lover, dead or alive, and take him home.

Once they got good and drunk – quietly so, but perceptibly vague and loose in their movements – the men threw their arms around each others' shoulders and danced heavily in a wide circle. They grunted to the rhythm of a single drum and pounded their bare feet against the earth in the same heavy cadence. Some of the men wept. Some looked lost in a stupor. This was a death dance, she knew. They were saying good-bye to their friends. They had grown up together in a society closer than so-called civilized people would ever know. Their friends did not include unreal non-people on television. They did not know people by e-mail and telephone. Since birth they had shared their houses, shared their food, slept in hammocks so close they could hear each other breathe, personally witnessed every birth and death in the village. Now they were going to see each other die.

After the dance, they took up their bows and arrows. They dipped the arrows in a gourd full of poison. It had to be terribly poisonous because a few ounces of the stuff was enough for hundreds of arrows. Ysa wondered if there was any cure for it. She wondered which was more deadly, a bullet or a nick with a poisoned arrow. She was almost glad she'd be curing bullet wounds. At least a bullet could be dug out of a wound. Poison could not. She wondered how the poison would wraps its tentacles around a body and drag it into death, whether the process would be slow and painful or quick and anesthetic. It wouldn't have surprised her if that death was better than death by bullet wound.

As soon as each man had his arrows ready, he jogged down a path into the forest. Ronsh was the last to go. With just a tilt of his head he motioned for Ysa to precede him. He said nothing when Soong Tan went before her, and Ysa said nothing when she saw that the girl was carrying her bow and half a dozen arrows.

They jogged at an easy pace, following a line of nearly naked men that wound into the dark forest. Their tight, brown bottoms looked as smooth and hairless as a child's. No one spoke, and the pace never slackened below a comfortable jog. Soong Tan kept up better than Ysa would have expected. Twice they stopped briefly. At a signal Ysa never heard, everyone simply halted and sank into a deep squat. No one spoke. They seemed to slip into a state of meditation, perhaps caused by the brew they had drunk, perhaps the result of centuries of long hunts in the forest. Too soon they rose and set off at the same easy jog.

They stopped for lunch, too – if you call a handful of cold, boiled manioc lunch. The gourd of jungle brandy came back down the line for a quick swallow by everyone except Ysa and Soong Tan. Then they set off again, padding quietly under the darkening canopy of distant leaves. She sensed a darkening of the sky and heard muffled thunder. Ysa tried to guess how far they had come. If they'd been running four miles an hour, they might have covered fifteen or twenty miles.

She smelled campfire smoke well before the man in front of her signaled for silence and a slower pace. The light of a clearing dappled the dark foliage. She and Soong Tan followed him as he crept off the path and into a low, dense thicket of ferns, vines and low plants. They passed several dozen men crouched among the leaves. The striped paint on their brown skin blended in with the foliage. She wished she could be as invisible, and with that thought she realized, fully, for the first time, the gulf between her and Soong Tan, who looked more like an Indian or forest animal than a sixth-grader from Beauville Elementary School. She wondered if she would ever get Soong Tan back or if the girl would forever remain an Indian.

Once they found the end of the line of warriors, they crept forward to the edge of the clearing. The scene shocked her. For some reason she felt she was looking over the brim of Hell itself. Beneath a colossal black cloud, a vast, uneven area lay as naked as a turbulent sea. The remains of its trees, broken field of stumps and branches, lay like the bodies across the scene of a massacre. Only a few muddy bulldozer trails cut through the crumpled debris. The dead branches looked like a tangle of giant skeletons. The trails led downward to a river. The camp and a single tree stood there as if ready to flee. Gradually Ysa pieced together the shacks, the movements of men, a tiny, colorful square – an inflatable boat perhaps – at the edge of the river, a long apparatus which looked to be a saw mill. Yes, as she strained her ears, she could hear its steel wheel spinning, a thin whine against the low growl of a gasoline generator. A skittish wind tossed the sound around as it swirled up leaves and dust.

Ysa whispered to Soong Tan, "Can one of those bows shoot that far?" The closest person was a good hundred meters away, maybe more.

"I think the big ones could," Soong Tan whispered back. "But I don't know how accurate it would be."

Ysa unslung her medical kit and extracted her little binoculars. The little lenses thrust her forward, all but putting her inside the camp. She saw the inflatable boat at the edge of the river. She saw the men under the tree, two on the ground – one perhaps a woman – and half a dozen standing around them. It was odd to see them shouting but to hear only distant voices floating on the odd, upswirling wind. She saw the saw mill, its wheel a blur, and beside it, incredibly, a man in jeans embracing a woman who was nude except for a pair of panties that looked like something off a battle tank. Their bodies were so close they blended into one. Their kiss seemed interminable as they frantically caressed each other, fluttering their hands over each others' bodies as if they had but moments to live. Two men held rifles on them. It didn't make sense. Was the couple being forced to make love standing up during an oncoming thunderstorm in the middle of a jungle clearing littered neck-deep with dead branches? Or were they making love despite the men with the rifles? Were they saying good-bye?

As she watched, something sparked inside her. It felt a lot like desire. The man's hands, the way they slid up and down the woman's spine, worked at her shoulders, groped around her waist, probed into her panties – they reminded her so much of Kit. How she longed for those hands! She wanted them all over her body in their hungry, seeking way. She wanted to feel them out of her control, out of his control, scurrying like animals too frenzied to know whether they wanted to flee or consume the flesh across which they so voraciously roamed. Watching so closely through the binoculars, she could almost feel those hands strong, thick-veined fingers taking her flesh for themselves. Though far from those hands, her own skin tingled with a distant memory brought close. She could not help but murmur, "Oh, Kit...Oh, Kit..."

"What's that?" Soong Tan asked. "What do you see?"

She had no words to explain to a child the passion she was seeing and feeling. To avoid answering, she almost said, "Nothing," but that would have been a lie too powerful to speak. Her lips moved as if kissing the air, but they formed no words.

"Let me see," Soong Tan shouted in a whisper, reaching for the binoculars.

Ysa could not release them. The vision held her captive. The kiss continued and intensified. The woman held the man's head in both hands as her mouth gobbled and sucked at his. He, impassioned beyond all restraint, squeezed and lifted her little bottom as if he might bring it up to his face. As if to help, as if to climb him, she wrapped her thin, muscular leg around his. Ysa could all but smell his sweat and feel his urgency against her.

A strange and terrifying sensation swept over Ysa. Just as the monstrous cloud had buried the sun, She became aware of herself in the forest looking into a clearing. It felt as if she were peering from a cave. Ensconced in the jungle, she was in prehistoric times with prehistoric people on a prehistoric mission. In the clearing was the twentieth century – a vast devastation of nature, a field of skeletal remains, the machinery of destruction. In the center of it all, under threat of annihilation, a man and a woman, an island unto themselves, clung to each other in desperation. In that field of death, their only hope was in each other, and the link between them was their nature, their passion, the last thing they would ever surrender to the twentieth century.

She lost them in a blur of tears. The scene before her, and the battle about to take place, reeled with apocalyptic grandness and complexity. Something great was taking place, something beyond her understanding. Her tears came in a confusion of fear, smallness and odd joy. Her soul reached out to the man and woman. She felt their solitude and their union.

She wiped her tears on the short sleeve of her T-shirt. Soong Tan, her little mouth agape with wonder, saw but said nothing. When Ysa returned the binoculars to her eyes, the significance and symbolism of the scene in the clearing grew even larger. The kiss had gone beyond the toleration of the men with the rifles. One unsheathed a machete, approached the couple and, smiling with cruelty, slowly sliced the blade between them, starting at the forehead, gradually peeling them apart. He didn't cut them – not their physical bodies, anyway. He just wedged the gray steel blade between their lips. As the lips parted, the blade descended to force their bodies apart. The woman leaned away as it passed her nipples, and then Ysa saw that the man was her man, her Kit, and the woman was Gaia, goddess of the trees and porpoises.

Before she knew what to feel, even before she had gasped with shock, she saw Kit's face snap into a blind rage. His teeth at a murderous angle, he hit the man with a fist as hard and quick as a cannonball. The man lifted off the ground and crumpled backward to the ground. In the same second, however, the other man hit Kit from behind, pounding his skull with the butt of his rifle. Kit collapsed to the ground.

Ysa was already snapping her fingers at Soon Tang when the man grabbed Gaia with one arm. The other arm still held the rifle while his friend crushed Gaia against himself , His black-whiskered face pursued her for a kiss. Ysa could see her wailing and pounding on the man. He seemed to enjoy her fear. Ysa knew exactly how Gaia felt. She'd been there before, under the crush of a cruel man. Her empathy overwhelmed her unformed anger at the kiss.

Soong Tan was still agape at the mystery.

"Quick," Ysa said in a voice as sharp as steel. "An arrow. Put an arrow down there."

"Where?" The girl was already stringing up one of her long, thin arrows. "It's too far to hit anything."

"Just come close. Look..." She handed over the binoculars. Soong Tan, the bow and arrow in one hand, scanned quickly. Ysa crouched beside her, pointing.

"Down low, up from the river, just above that shack. See the man with the woman?"

"It's Gaia!"

"Damn right. Put an arrow as close as you can. But don't hit Kit."

"Kit? Is that Kit?"

"On the ground. Right. For God sake's don't hit him."

Without taking her eyes from the target, Soong Tan passed over the binoculars. She set an arrow in the bow and aimed it high. "If I aim right at him, I'm bound to miss," she said.

Before Ysa could unscramble the logic of that tactic, Soong Tan released the arrow. With a muffled tick, it disappeared from the bow. Soong Tan snatched back the binoculars. Ysa's heart froze mid-beat until the girl whispered, "Yes."

Her hands to her face as if to pray, Ysa asked, "What did you hit?"

"A log. Of course. It's all logs down there."

"And what happened?" Ysa squinted hard at the distant figures.

"The man saw it. He's looking this way."

"And Gaia?"

"He let her go. He threw her on the ground. She's crawling to Kit..."

"That bitch!"

"Want me to shoot her?" She sounded so eager!

"No!" Ysa was crying now. "No...I don't know what. I don't know..."

Suddenly Ronsh was standing over her. In a harsh whisper he shouted angry words in Munducuru. Ysa saw him wanting to kick her, smack her, barely holding himself back. His war paint glowed. She smelled the strong wine on his breath and saw it in his angry eyes, glassy and red with drink.

"What's he saying?" she pleaded to Soong Tan.

"I think he said he's really pissed off about something."

"Watch your language, young lady."

"You're not my mother."

"And it's a good thing!" She shifted to Portuguese. "Ronsh, what is the problem?"

"We are not ready for the attack!" he growled. "Now they know we are here!"

As soon as he said it, a rifle shot rang out, then another. As if in response, thunder exploded. Still, no rain fell. The wind was eerily dry but smelling of rain. Ronsh rushed away, urging the men to get up and follow him. More rifle shots sent bullets ticking through the leaves. Single file, keeping low, the Indians moved downhill along the edge of the clearing. Ysa pulled Soong Tan to the ground. The gourd of herbal wine was beside them, tipped to its side, empty.

"We're in trouble, girl."

"What do you men we, Keemosabee?"

Ysa looked deep into the war-painted face of her little green-eyed half-sister. For a solid second she thought the girl was serious. Then Soong Tan broke into a gap-toothed grin and wrapped her arms around Ysa's head. "Don't worry," she cooed. "This is nothing for a couple of mean chicks like us."

God bless the child. She infused Ysa with quiet confidence. Yes, they would get out of this. It was just a matter of thinking things out, moving fast, not making mistakes. First thing they had to do was reach Kit.

Then she realized the people under the tree were Edgar and Elizama. She scrutinized them through the binoculars. Yes, there was his goddam gumball machine, right next to a...coffin. What the hell was going on down there?

Elizama was helping Edgar up off the ground. He looked bruised but not badly injured. Ysa had to scan all over the camp before she found Kit and Gaia wiggling through the mud like a couple of reptiles in rut. There were heading for the river. The loggers had taken up defensive positions near their huts. They shot into the forest in blind fear. Kit and Gaia would have to pass them. The clutter of branches might provide them enough cover to get through. They'd be pretty safe until they reached the open ground at the river.

Edgar and Elizama were heading for the river, too. Absurdly, Edgar was taking his gumball machine, rolling it before him like a log. They didn't crawl combat-style like Kit and Gaia. They just ducked down and waddled. The machine didn't roll straight, so they had to keep making mid-stream corrections. They looked like they might be out of sight of the loggers. They advanced slowly but had a head start over Kit and Gaia. They didn't yet know they were in a race. Whoever got to the river first could get away in the inflatable boat. It could hold two and maybe three, but definitely not four and a gumball machine.

The first arrows were lobbing into the loggers' circle from several directions. They weren't hitting anybody, but they were coming close. The gunfire intensified. Kit, following Gaia, kept pushing her ahead. Mud covered both of them. She kept hesitating and he kept shoving. They were reaching the point where they'd have to break and run across a hundred yards of open land. They'd be running downhill, but the loggers, if they felt like wasting a couple of bullets, could easily pick them off. Instead of dashing into the open, however, Kit and Gaia turned toward the loggers and the huts. By this time, Edgar and Elizama were almost at the boat. Kit and Gaia disappeared behind a hut.

"Oh...my...God," Ysa gasped.

"What? What?" Soong Tan pulled at the binoculars.

"I don't believe it."

"What?"

She held the binoculars to Soong Tan's eyes but did not let go of them.

"Is that them?"

Them was a couple of upside-down coffins creeping along the ground like monstrous bugs. Kit no doubt inhabited the larger one, Gaia the smaller. They bumped along, tilting down the hill, following the deep tracks the bulldozer had left from pulling logs to the river. Ysa and Soong Tan took turns yanking the binoculars from each other to follow the action.

It didn't take the loggers long to notice. Their gunfire turned to send a few slugs into the coffins. The coffins stopped dead. But then they started moving again, skittering fast on invisible legs. Then arrows started coming down on them, too.

Down below, at the river, Edgar and Elizama were trying to get their gumball machine into the boat. It wasn't working. They had tipped the machine into the water and were trying to lift it up and in. It was longer than the boat, however, so as soon as they release it, it rolled off. Now it was in the water. They needed both their hands to lift it up, but as soon as they let go of the boat, it floated out of reach. The water was rising and turning muddy, probably from the storm that was coming in from upstream. When Edgar splashed over to grab the boat, the gumball machine started to float away, pulling Elizama with it. Then an arrow swooped in. It chunked into the muddy bank and stood there like a new-grown sapling. Then a swarm of bullets hit the water in neat, vicious blips. When Edgar looked up and saw the coffins coming, he started moving very fast. Elizama, stumbling around in the water like a terrified antelope, churned up so much splash that they were probably hard to target.

Soong Tan noticed the fire first. It was already rearing up at the far end of the clearing, slightly higher in elevation than the camp. Its flames burned with an especially hot orange. Sparks gushed into the air like a perverted waterfall that had turned to fire and flowed upward. The wind from the thundercloud sucked the fire higher, even lifted small burning branches into the air.

"They're going to burn the whole thing," Ysa said.

"There's more over there." Soong Tan pointed to the other side of the clearing. "We'd better get out of here."

Ysa couldn't tear her eyes from the scene at the river. Just as Edgar got the gum machine balanced on the boat, Kit rolled it off. Edgar shoved Kit. Kit shoved Edgar. Elizama joined the fray. Gaia just climbed into the boat.

"They can't see the fire," Ysa snapped. "They don't have long to get out of there." A hailstorm of bullets was slicing up the water. The only escape was the boat. Kit and Edgar fought. Kit was obviously restraining himself. If he hadn't, Edgar would already have been dead. But they were virtually brothers. It wasn't the kind of fight that Kit could end quickly.

Elizama dragged her soaking body into the boat. She had no

idea how to row. Gaia grabbed one oar. Elizama held onto the other and wouldn't let it go. They both rowed like mad. The boat swirled in a circle, moving upstream and down as Kit and Edgar worked things out in an equally disorganized way. They didn't seem to notice the arrows and bullets there were missing them by only a few yards.

"Those idiots are going to get killed,:" Ysa moaned. "We've got to do something." She passed Soong Tan the binoculars and tumbled forward into the clearing.

"No!' Soong Tan shouted. "Ysa, they'll kill you!"

But she didn't hear. Stumbling toward the river, she screamed to Kit and pointed wildly toward the fire. But the storm and the roar of the fire and the gunshots pummeled her voice. Soong Tan shrieked after her, but Ysa kept going. She was barely conscious of herself as she dashed into the clearing. The only thing in her mind was the need to warn Kit, to save him. She did not notice when the gunfire, unable to find Indians, turned on her. The cliff of flames towered behind her, advancing like a volcanic avalanche. Smoke swirled around her, masking her from the gunfire but only to save her for a more painful death. Still, she kept going, leaping through the tangle of branches with a fleetness she never would have thought possible.

Soong Tan saw the danger, and she saw the arrows sail in at Ysa, long shots from far away. That Indians must have been completely schnockered if they thought they could hit her. It didn't even make sense that they were shooting. They probably thought she was defecting to the side of the whites. So it was a combination of stupidity and luck that one arrow, from over a hundred yards away, sailing through buffeting winds of heat and storm found its way to Ysa. To her, it just seemed to appear in her thigh. As calmly as could be, she plucked it out, held it before her face, examined its slim tip. It was just a little tooth, small but needle-sharp. The wound was less than an inch deep. How silly, she thought. What a silly weapon. It didn't even hurt. Lost in a fog of incomprehension, she lifted the arrow for Kit to see. But Kit, of course, had no idea she was anywhere in that neck of the jungle. He was still thrashing around with Edgar.

It took Ysa several seconds to realize why the arrow wound didn't hurt. By the time she sensed the numbness spreading up her thigh, a sudden dizziness threw her to the ground. She came to the earth with an odd sense of relief. Though it was within her arms, as warm and welcome as a mother, the planet looked distant. It floated away from her even as she hugged it.

Soong Tan saw the arrow and knew immediately that Ysa had little time to live. As if she'd been trained for the situation, she reached for the gourd the men had left behind. She shook it. It sloshed a bit. They hadn't drunk it all. It was the only hope.

Like all small children, she knew fear very well. She also knew, with unquestioned certainty, that she was immortal. The bullets and arrows would not touch her. The fire would back off. If worst came to worst, she would just rise into the air, lifted by the hand of God, and all would be taken care of. So she tucked the gourd under her little arm and launched herself into the clearing. From a distance, she must have looked like a weasel working its way over and under branches, popping up in unexpected places, ducking down again, sneaking forward, stopping at nothing. She supposed they were shooting at her, but she couldn't really tell. It didn't matter. She

"Then how come so many people all dying?"

"I asked the same question. They say it doesn't cure White Man's diseases."

"I bet it doesn't cure bullet wounds too well, either."

The Indians were going to attack the logging camp. Their mission was double. They wanted to kill the loggers who were killing the forest, and they wanted to capture the amoebiasis medicine. If they managed to steal some equipment, too, that would be good, but mostly they just wanted to wipe out the encampment.

They knew their bows and arrows would confront firearms, but as Indians saw it, they could die by fighting or by waiting for disease and starvation. Ysa had not been privy to the discussions that led to the decision to attack. Apparently they'd been thinking about it for a long time. In fact, the discussions were still going on, now under the influence of strong herbal wine. Ysa could understand none of it besides the general gist. The gist was they were scared but they knew what they had to do.

Ysa was to accompany them as medic. When somebody got hurt, she was supposed to heal them. With what, she did not know. She had her medical kit. She could wrap a bandage, possibly stitch together a wound, maybe, just maybe remove a bullet from a shallow wound. But she had no anesthesia, no antiseptic, nothing with which to sterilize instruments, no antibiotics, to real surgical instruments other than a single scalpel and several clamps. She wondered whether her medical work would help or hurt.

She also wondered which side she was on. Certainly she sympathized with the Indians, but the loggers were just men, workers glad to have a job. The real culprits lived far away, in Brazil's big cities, would reach Ysa. If they shot her after that, well, so what?

She reached Ysa, but not in time. She was unconscious, unresponsive, her eyes neither closed nor open. That was when Soong Tan started crying. The sting of the smoke and the tears blinded her. She pulled Ysa into her lap, forced a finger into her mouth, pried it open a bit and tilted the gourd to Ysa's lips. The dregs of the wine gurgled out. It drained through her teeth and washed over her face. Nothing happened. Ysa didn't even cough. Nothing.

The fire seemed to have seen them. It was coming fast. It sounded angry, as if looking for the culprit who had slain the forest. It saw Ysa and Soong Tan among the dead trees and stormed toward them. The heat began to hurt. The only thing Soong Tan could think to do was grab Ysa by the shoulders of her shirt and drag her downhill toward the river. She got the body to the bulldozer trail. From there she could pull with one arm while the other reached ahead to claw at the mud. Gravity helped, but the mud pulled at the inert weight. If she had not reached an unexpected steep decline, she would not have kept ahead of the flames. Ysa's body slid down, mercilessly quick until they came to a rut almost as deep as Soong Tan was tall. There was no way to go further. It was there that she gave up. Almost unconscious from the smoke, she buried her head in Ysa's chest, and the last thing she remembered was the sensation of great comfort she found there.

She did not feel or remember the strong hands that grabbed her and Ysa by their hair. She did not remember being dragged through the mud. She did not know she was in a coffin until she awoke. Consciousness came slowly, a floating back to the world accompanied by the sweetest sound in the world, a soft gurgle of water against wood.

Above her, the sky, so blue, so blue, shimmered with sunlight. She was in Heaven, floating on a cloud. Only after a full minute did she realize that she did not want to be there, not alone. Then, absurdly, yet in a way logically, quite dreamlike, a little airplane the color of a taxi flew by, purring as it passed.

When she tried to sit up, the cloud beneath her rocked violently. She grabbed the horizon that encircled her and rose to look beyond it. She gasped to see herself in a river, right down at water level. Kit sat few feet away, inhabiting another coffin as if it were no more than a bathtub. He was leaning back, hands behind his head, looking up at the sky, ruminating with a distant thought.

And then she heard the voice of an angel...the voice of Ysa, right behind her. She, too, sat in a coffin, hers just a bit smaller than Kit's. Not far beyond them, the globe of a gumball machine bobbed in the water, glinting in the sun. "Good morning, Soong Tan," Ysa sang. "I hope you slept well."

Soong Tan had to draw a careful breath before she could speak. She said, "Are we dead?"

Kit and Ysa laughed. "No," Kit said, voice full of joy. "We are not dead. We are alive. Very, very, very much alive."

With quick little hand-paddles, Ysa maneuvered her macabre canoe closer to Soong Tan's. Careful not to tip, she reached out and took Soong Tan's hand. It was warm, dry and still weak from sleep. "We thought you might like to know," she said. "As soon as we get back to civilization, Kit and I are getting married."

Soong Tan's face flew open with surprise. "He proposed?"

"From a coffin, no less. I suspect that's a first."

"And you said yes?"

"As a matter of fact I did." She smiled a bit shyly, wondering why it felt so strange to report this development to a kid.

"Big mistake," Soong Tan said, smiling.

Kit seemed to know what she meant. "Naw," he said as he drifted close enough to take Ysa's other hand. "If we can survive the Amazon, we can survive marriage."

"Sounds too civilized to me." Soong Tan cinched her eyebrows down toward the top of her nose. "I think it could lead to trouble."

Kit let loose a laugh so loud it seemed to throw back the jungle from the bank of the river. "And I think it could lead to a definite improvement in civilization," he said. "I think it's about time civilization found out what love's all about.

And with that, he tilted his head back and inflated the biggest gum bubble in the world, a thin-skinned balloon precisely the color of the sky back home in Virginia.

Epilogue

Ysa, Soong Tan and Kit just floated with the flow until they came to the old man's house where Ysa, Soong Tan, and Ronsh had spent a night. He put them in a canoe and paddled them to Jacaréacanga, where he was highly rewarded. There they learned that Edgar, Elizama and Gaia had returned in their little yellow plane. They had reported the battle at the logging camp, the fire, and the certain deaths of three Americans. Then they chartered a plane back to Belém.

Kit, Ysa and Soong Tan left the same way. In Belém, without bothering the call Edgar and Elizama to thank them for a very nice time, they grabbed the first plane to Rio and from there the first plane to Washington, D.C. When Susan called from the airport, she was surprised, to say the least. Last she'd heard, from the U.S. consulate in Belém, they were dead. Passport records named her their next of kin. She was supposed to fill out a form and have it notarized if she wanted their bodies searched for and returned – at her expense. She was still thinking about it when their bodies phoned from Dulles International. Ysa says, "Hello, Susan, we're back.

Could you come pick us up?"

She sure could.

It took two weeks to bring them back to official life. Because the consulate had reported them dead, they were dead. Two checks for half a million dollars each arrived in their mailbox – their life insurance pay-off. Kit called the insurance company and tried to give it back, but they wouldn't take it until he proved he wasn't dead. So he decided to prove it by cashing the checks, but by the time he got to the bank, they'd been canceled. So, just as Elizama had predicted, he and Ysa were dead and rich – for a little while, anyway.

Their deaths also delayed their marriage. Until the whole mess got straightened out, they had to wait. But they've picked a date for the big event. The only question is where to do it. Soong Tan says not in a church, no way. Kit says not at City Hall, no way. Ysa thinks maybe Africa would be a good place to get married, maybe out in the Serengeti near a herd of wildebeests. Kit says maybe. Soong Tan says there's no maybe about it. She's ready to go.

Kit did some roaming around the Internet. He found an Associated Press report of several Indian uprisings, not just near Jacaréacanga but throughout Amazonia. Gold miners and loggers were fleeing like rats from a firestorm. The report didn't mention whether they were chewing gum when they emerged from the jungle. The news never made it to any headlines, at least not in the United States. Ysa never learned whether the Indians got their medicine. It didn't seem to matter. If they had managed to oust civilization from their territory, they had solved their fundamental problem. As long as civilization didn't get in their way, they'd get by just as they had since the Stone Age.

Kit opened up his ice cream stand just in time for the summer rush. Ysa showed up at her lab a little late. They weren't too sure they still had a job for her, but when she offered them a very impressive collection of stool samples replete with tropical microbes, in the interest of science they let her in. Soong Tan went back to school. To make up for her excessive absence, they had her write a long essay about her vacation. She wrote forty-eight pages. "I went to the Amazon," she wrote. "It was pretty cool."

About the Author

Glenn Alan Cheney is a writer, translator, painter, and managing editor of New London Librarium. The topics of his nonfiction books include Chernobyl, the Pilgrims, Abraham Lincoln, Amazonia, environmental issues, nuns, Brazil's Quilombo dos Palmares, the Estrada Real, cats, bees, death and burial, the end of the world, incarceration, Mohandas Gandhi, nuclear proliferation, and teen addiction, as well as a few novels and a book of poetry. He has translated Brazilian classics by Machado de Assis and Rubem Alves. He lives with his wife, Solange Aurora, in Hanover, Conn.

New London Librarium

New London Librarium is a literary press that specializes in publishing books that are unlikely to attain the sales expected by larger publishers. It publishes series on Catholic issues, Brazil, art, history, current controversies, and translations. For more information, see NLLibrarium.com\

www.ingramcontent.com/pod-product-compliance
Lightning Source LLC
Chambersburg PA
CBHW030520310726
48979CB00010B/1736/J

* 9 7 8 1 9 4 7 0 7 4 6 1 3 *